'But, Scott. . .'

'Look, Victoria, I ca[...]
felt through a doze[...]
you might decide later that living up here is not
your scene—'

Suddenly she was furiously angry. 'Do you
think,' she asked him through clenched teeth,
'that after knowing you I would ever think of
leaving? You're being stupid, Scott, to equate
one woman's views and desires with another's.'

Dear Reader

This month, I would like to ask you to think about the kind of heroine you would like to find in our stories. Do you think she should be sweet and gentle, on the look-out for a man who will be able to care for and nurture her, or should the heroine be able to give as good as she gets, throwing punch for punch, and quite capable of standing up for herself? If you have any opinions on this matter please let us know, so that we can continue to give you the books you want to read!

The Editor

Mons Daveson is Australian, living on Queensland's Sunshine Coast. Her family has now grown up and left home, giving her more time to write. She sets her books mainly in Australia although she has ventured to other exotic locations such as Egypt, used for her book MY LORD KASEEM.

MASTER OF NAMANGILLA

BY

MONS DAVESON

MILLS & BOON LIMITED
ETON HOUSE   18–24 PARADISE ROAD
RICHMOND   SURREY   TW9 1SR

*First published in Great Britain in 1991
by Mills & Boon Limited*

© Mons Daveson 1991

*Australian copyright 1991
Philippine copyright 1993
This edition 1993*

ISBN 0 263 77759 6

*Set in Linotron Plantin 10 on 12 pt
01-9308-55609*

Made and printed in Great Britain

CHAPTER ONE

THE girl leaned out of the window of her compartment, wondering why the train, which had been rushing so forcefully through the long dark night, had come to a hissing standstill. She saw that they were stationary in a wide, empty countryside—the only sign of civilisation being a big, tall water tank. Seeing the guard passing by, she called softly, 'Will we be here for long?'

'About ten minutes or so,' he answered curtly, as he continued on towards the engine.

Victoria glanced at the recumbent figure in the other bunk who was still making the noise which had awoken her, then with decision reached for her jeans to pull over her pyjama bottoms. Moving quietly, she walked the two short steps along the corridor to the outside door and opened it. Leaving it swinging wide, she jumped down.

Hands in pockets, head raised to a diamond-studded sky, she strolled a few yards alongside the stationary train, enjoying the cool fresh breeze that was wafting against her, carrying its tang of the bushland.

She went only a few yards, keeping her open door in sight. She didn't see the four laughing young men jump down behind her as she passed, or the other solitary man even further behind, who had spoken to the guard and then stood beside his compartment on the silent, deserted railway siding.

'And what's a pretty girl like you doing walking about by herself? We've come to keep you company.'

Startled, Victoria swung round. Her accosters were

5

laughing and seemed ordinary young men—but they had been drinking and were from a sitting car further along.

She said pleasantly, making a move to walk back through them to her own carriage, 'I came out for a breath of air. I'm going back now.'

'Oh, don't go yet,' came from the large burly one who was closest to her, as he reached out a long arm to swing her against him.

As his head came down, she flung up her free arm to guard her face while saying coldly, 'Don't be silly. I'm going back to the train.'

She wasn't frightened. . .yet. But she was beginning to be. No sign of life came from the train near them, and there was just open deserted countryside around.

She heard only excited laughter greet her words, and as a second body crowded closer, its hand going out to catch her guarding arm, she did become frightened, and began to hit wildly at it.

The other passenger standing further along hesitated for a fraction of a second, then with the faintest shrug of wide shoulders walked with long strides to reach the group.

The flat of one hand pushed, and a body staggered back. Then iron-hard fingers closed on the arm imprisoning the girl, swinging her captor round.

Furious now at having what was meant to be only a laughing game interrupted, the would-be Don Juan started forward, fist raised. Then he stopped dead, suddenly sobered.

The newcomer had pushed back the big hat he was wearing, and starshine struck pinpoints of brilliance from eyes looking directly at them. The brightness showed, too, the absolute assurance of ability emanating from the motionless figure.

'I'd return to the train if I were you,' a cold astringent

voice was telling them; but for a timeless second they stood, four men facing the one beside her. Then they were edging round and moving towards their own compartment.

'And as for you,' that cold voice was continuing curtly, 'why go walking by yourself in a place like this, at this time of night?' A hand was sweeping out to indicate the deserted bushland about them; the long line of the sleeping train with only its quietly hissing engine disturbing the silence of the night. He said again in that soft contemptuous tone, 'Haven't you any sense at all?'

'Oh, yes, I have sense.' In a tone as cold as his own, but shaking with either anger or delayed fright, the girl answered. 'But how was I to know that in my own country—my civilised country—it wouldn't be safe to walk without a mob of hooligans attacking me? I've lived in a city all my life and never had such a thing happen. . .'

But she found her words wasted effort as the man took hold of her arm to hurry her—and none too gently either—along the empty platform to where the door of her carriage was swinging wide. Furiously she jerked it free, hating that surge of electricity sweeping through her at his touch, at this reaction to the disagreeable scene of a minute ago.

Handing her up steps with the white first-class stamp blazoned beside them, the stranger told her—and that cold, curt tone he had used throughout had changed now to a silken softness that set her teeth on edge—'It's rich, spoilt city girls like you, who think they can behave as they like, and have thought only for themselves, who create trouble wherever they go. No girl from up here would act in such an irresponsible manner——'

Interrupting him, not with silken softness however but with cold, deliberate anger, Victoria answered, 'I am not rich! And I am not spoilt! Also, I have a right to walk where I please, at any time I choose. And if the men up here,' the tone her voice carried as she uttered the last few words was quite as contemptuous as the one he had been using, 'can only get their kicks in behaving like that. . .'

Her diatribe trailed off as she found herself being pushed through the carriage doorway, and involuntarily she snatched back the arm he had taken to do the pushing. On the steps, she turned to look at him, their faces now on the same level. However, his features were hidden by the big slouched hat, while her own were outlined as she faced the illumination of starshine.

His hand swung the door shut, and the voice said, still carrying that silken softness, 'They were only out for a bit of fun. . .but women like you carry trouble around with them. I don't know why I bothered.'

'Why did you, then?' She was answering hotly, but she found herself speaking to empty space. Through the glass pane she saw only a shadow moving along the line of dark carriages; she saw him climb through a door further along, and it seemed immediately that the train was moving, gathering speed quickly as if it had waited long enough.

In her compartment, her jeans were swiftly shrugged off, and, thankfully noting that her fellow traveller had turned over and was sleeping quietly now, Victoria climbed into her bunk.

She lay for a long time, listening to the clickety-clack of the wheels speeding the miles behind them as she endeavoured to clear from her mind all thoughts of the last half-hour. She succeeded. For when at last she slipped into the oblivion of sleep, both the figures of that drinking quartet and that other disagreeable man—all of whom she would never see again—had disappeared from her memory.

A day and a half later, she found she had more important things to occupy her mind—the first one being how in the name of goodness she could get out of this situation she had so stupidly got herself into. Because as she said a curt thank-you to the young man now placing her suitcases just inside the door, she realised how silly she had been.

'You're welcome,' replied this son of the station's manager, but his sidelong glance belied the words. And his look had been justified, she knew, as she watched him depart—brown-haired and young, with hazel eyes. He also had what she supposed was the easy, loping walk of a man continually in the saddle. Victoria was suddenly ashamed of her behaviour.

She crossed the lino-covered floor, her glance dismissing the austere room about her. There was a bed covered with an old-fashioned candlewick spread. There was a dressing-table and wardrobe, of the same antiquity. She sighed and continued on to the window.

An aura of dismay seemed to encircle the young figure, outlined though it was in brilliant sunshine. In the crumpled jeans and shirt in which she had travelled, she appeared almost too slight. Her hair, like that of the man who had just departed, was brown also, albeit fairer, and it swung free about her shoulders. Gazing unhappily from the face it surrounded, dark grey eyes looked over a gorge into the infinity of distance.

Her father had been right—as usual. A sardonic smile twisted her lips as she remembered the right royal row that had swirled around their two figures that evening. For you didn't argue with her father. A top surgeon, he was deferred to always. Still, she had made herself go on.

'Look, Dad,' she had broken in, trying to get her point across, 'I'm not book-clever like Mark and Irene. You should be satisfied with them. What's the good of my going back to the university next year? I might get my degree. . .but I am *not* going back. Let me go down to Uncle Luke's for a time to get myself sorted out.'

'Victoria, that station is miles away from anywhere. What in the name of goodness will you do up there—or who would you ever meet?'

'Oh, come on, George! That's my home you're talking about,' her mother chimed in gently, hating all this upset. 'And look who I met!'

'Yes, my dear, and so you did. But it was only that I called in with a friend while passing through. It might easily not have happened.'

'Well, I don't want to meet anybody. I've met plenty of men these last two years. . .and partied, and sailed with them. Meeting more at the present time is the last thing on my agenda. Look, Dad,' Victoria told him again, 'I'd like to go to Uncle Luke for a few months, ride with him and help with the stock. He always needs a helping hand, you know. And then we'll see. I'm just tired of studying.' Weariness had coloured the young voice.

'Very well.' Her father had thrown up both arms and stalked away.

However, at this moment, looking at the scene outspread so far below, Victoria laughed abruptly, accepting now that he had probably been right—again. Still, for the time being, here she was after almost three days of travelling, the last half-one at least being accomplished in the luxury of a big Jaguar. For her mother's friend had been waiting to welcome her as she stepped down from the rattling train at a ghost town called Chillagoe.

Oh, well. . . She drew a deep breath, and, turning away from a window that seemed to perch on the edge of the world, she crossed to her suitcase and snapped open the locks.

And a few minutes later, as she entered the big kitchen, washed and brushed free of dust from the long journey, Mrs Leith told her, 'This is Geoffrey, Victoria.'

'Hi,' she greeted him, returning the same sort of smile he was extending to her. Apparently he was as little enamoured with this arrangement as she was beginning to be—fourteen years old, spoilt by the look of things, managing to avoid boarding-school because he hadn't wanted to go, and now it had suddenly hit Mrs Leith that times were changing. Victoria glanced from the dejected, freckled face of the boy to the figure of his mother, who sat at the head of the large table. She was ramrod-straight, with salt and pepper hair cut severely short, and Victoria thought she seemed so much a part of this unsettled far northern country, so different from her own mother's gentleness and dependence. Both from station backgrounds, they had attended the same boarding-school and had remained friends for always. And it had been her letter, arriving just after that furious quarrel with her father, that had made an undecided Victoria accept this teaching position Mrs Leith had asked her mother to arrange.

It would do just as well as Uncle Luke's, she had thought. And with the Queensland correspondence course for her to check with, teaching the young boy would be like falling off a log.

Again she found herself grinning wryly to herself. She had been well and truly hoist with her own petard. Still, she hadn't wanted to take that job of office receptionist her father had said later that he would find for her.

Her attention came back with a rush to the immediate present as her employer said briskly, 'Give Victoria her tea, Jennifer,' then added, 'My daughter, who left school last year and refuses to go on to something else; who also thinks she knows everything at eighteen!'

Another one, thought Victoria, while saying hello to the younger girl.

'Hi, there,' she received in return.

Jennifer brought her cup across the room, saying, 'I'll wait on you today, because you've only just arrived, but make the most of it, because it's not going to happen again.' The words might have been curt, but a smile accompanied them.

Friendly, careless, spoilt the same way as her brother was, by the sound of it, Victoria decided as she accepted both the greeting and her cup. She also decided quite definitely that she would have to find a way to get out of this mess she had got herself into. She jumped, literally, when Mrs Leith suddenly addressed her.

'You've taken on quite a job, Victoria. We're just beginning to realise up here in the bush that to run a station this size takes the knowledge and expertise that modern methods are opening up—and Geoffrey would never get into agricultural college as things are. I do know he should have been away at school, however. . .' Here Mrs Leith sighed before adding, 'So you see, I'm pinning all my hopes on you.'

What was she to answer? That incredibly long journey had seemed never-ending, and in far-away Brisbane Victoria had not realised that she would be this far out in the never-never. But. . .she *had* accepted the job. It *had* been her own decision. Oh, well, she would wait and see what tomorrow brought.

Her employer had glanced sharply at her as if noticing

her hesitation, but she only said as she began to pack crockery on a tray, 'Why don't you take Victoria outside, Jennifer, and show her around?'

Outside, they found that the fiery orb which had sent down its molten heat throughout the whole of their journey still showed it was a force to be reckoned with. But a breeze stirring through the trees from across the water sent its welcoming freshness to cool them as Jennifer stood deciding what to do.

'We'll go down and I'll show you the river first, Victoria,' she said, 'because it's the part of home I love best.'

They trod the wide steep steps which were cut into the hillside and that led down to the river so far below. Arriving breathless, Victoria unexpectedly found herself laughing, pleased that she had kept up with that quick-silver figure jumping down before her like an express train. It had been a frighteningly fast journey. But suddenly they were in deep shadows, sunlight cut off by the sheer cliff behind.

'Do you know, Jennifer,' she remarked, gazing at the slowly moving river, 'I really expected to have only a cup of water to wash in up here? The papers seem to be always screaming about drought in the cattle country—but there's all this!' She gestured towards the flat sheet of water.

'We are having a drought,' Jennifer told her. 'We're just lucky to have a river running through the property which hasn't quite dried up yet. But further out we're having to sink wells. And we don't have all the grass we need because of it, but Scott lets us have the use of some of his pastures. He has plenty, and water galore which he doesn't need—at least, not just yet.'

'Water galore! Isn't that like having gold in the outback? Doesn't this man run cattle on his station. . .?' Abruptly, Victoria's words trailed away, and she wondered why she bothered. What did she care about water—or even the outback?

'Yes, water does take the place of gold in this country, but Scott——' had a different nuance entered her companion's tone? '—didn't have much say in his station for a long while until these last few years, and it went to rack and ruin. So he doesn't have the stock it would be able to support.

'However, being poor in the sense of actual money doesn't matter up here. Many of the station-owners are in the same position while owning properties worth millions. And, of course, Scott's station is one of the best in the north!'

Here Jennifer paused for a moment, then slowly resumed, 'I don't know if I should mention this, but Mum will probably tell you to tread warily where Scott is concerned. The stories about him and his women keep the territory in ninety per cent of its gossip.'

'Oh, there are always stories, Jennifer,' Victoria answered, more than a little irritably. She wasn't interested in this local gossip; she certainly wouldn't be interested in this local Lothario, either. There had been more than enough of those—collected by her mother and invited along to parties which had been organised in an attempt to pair her off.

Jennifer had scooped up some pebbles and was shying them one at a time into the water. 'I know, Victoria,' she replied over her shoulder, 'that people like to talk, but up here no one would malign Scott. He was born here. . .he belongs! But even Uncle Pete, easygoing as he is, shrugs and says he shouldn't have allowed what his stepmother did to change him so drastically.

'Thank heavens he doesn't turn me on, probably because I'm already turned on by someone else. However, in that I'm one of the very few exceptions. We also know at home that for all his charm and charisma he cares for nothing except Namangilla. Still, that doesn't prevent him enjoying himself quite extensively. . .or so the gossip goes.'

'Well, here's one he won't be able to enjoy himself with,' muttered Victoria.

'Oh, look!' Suddenly Jennifer was not interested in gossip any longer. She shied the last pebble away, wiped her hands down the side of her shorts, and said, 'There's Jack, bringing a mob down to water.'

Relieved that this brought an end to a subject which was of no interest to her, Victoria turned to see a haze of dust moving towards them from the far side of the river. In the westering rays of a setting sun it took on a mystical, see-through look. Hand up, shading her eyes, she saw cattle in the mass for the first time, and the noise emanating from them made her thankful there was a river between. As she watched, however, order and quiet were emerging from chaos; the cattle were drinking.

For a brief moment through the obscuring haze a horse and rider showed, and from beside her echoed a loud 'coo. . .ee. . .eee!' Also from beside her, an arm was raised, beckoning.

Victoria caught the flash of white in an ebony face, as a 'Hi, Jen,' floated over the separating distance, and another arm was raised in answer.

On a pebbly white beach that fringed a placidly flowing river, with the pungent aroma of eucalyptus scenting the atmosphere all around them, they waited for the horseman. He arrived, hoofs sending sparkling droplets flying as he splashed through the shallows. Victoria moved rather nervously away from the animal as it curvetted and sidled closer to them. Again she saw the flash of white against black, then the face went grave as Jennifer introduced them.

'This is Victoria Steene, Jack. She's come to help Geoffrey get through his entrance exams.'

As he greeted her, the large-brimmed hat came off, then his attention returned to Jennifer as she asked, 'Are we getting ready to send cattle to the sales, Jack? I didn't think it was the time for it.'

'I don't think so. Mr Brown said to bring these away from the five-mile and settle them down here.' Then without any outside sign of direction his mount began to sidle back to the river, while he said over a shoulder, 'I'm off to the mission for the weekend, Jen. Any messages?'

The girl's hand was too casually laid on that restless beast, Victoria decided as she watched Jennifer walking beside it to the water's edge. Then, apparently with her questions answered, she just as casually slapped the flank of glistening hide beside her. Splashing their way back across the water, both forms were soon lost in the gathering dusk.

They also turned homewards, and suddenly Victoria was glad to leave this darkening, unfamiliar world behind; this primitive land that was so different from anything she had ever known.

She found the return journey more arduous than the descent had been, and as she paused once on the steep incline to catch her breath, a backward glance at the scene so far below showed her only muted colours. Trees along the waterway were merely shadows, the milling cattle blending into the coming night. The gleam of water was still there, but even as she looked the glimmer disappeared. Daylight had gone!

CHAPTER TWO

ENTERING the house by the back veranda, they stepped into another world. Modern civilisation was there in the warm brightly lit room with its smell of baking and the sound of voices echoing around it; with pressure lamps shedding their lights as brightly as any city electricity.

'Hi, Peter,' greeted Jennifer, and Victoria saw that the recipient of this welcome was the man who had carried her cases in. She smiled warmly at him, to make up for her earlier curtness.

Apparently he harboured no animosity, returning her smile with a friendly one of his own.

'Jack just brought a mob down to the river, Mum. Are we sending a train of beef into the sales?' asked Jennifer.

'No. For now, we're hanging on to our stock. We have enough grass and water for the time being, thank goodness.'

'He also told me he was going over to the mission for the weekend, and that he'd heard there might be a new doctor arriving to give old Dr Selwyn a helping hand.'

Marking the edge of a pie-crust with the prongs of a fork, her mother paused for a moment, then answered, 'I hadn't heard.' She continued, 'But as you know, it's holiday-time, and that often brings helping hands.' She went back to her pastry as if that closed the subject.

Then, as her daughter went to interrupt, she raised a hand to silence her. From outside echoed the rhythmical thud of hoofs travelling fast.

'That's Scott!' said Peter's voice with certainty. 'I'd recognise his way of riding anywhere.'

'Oh, no,' muttered Victoria to herself. She didn't want to meet anyone else tonight. All she desired was to go to bed and let oblivion wipe out a tiredness born of travelling all those hundreds of miles to reach this place. Miles that had also carried her into a totally new and alien environment. Still, she couldn't walk away from a dinner table just before the meal was ready to be set on it.

So she straightened her back, allowing indifference to colour her expression, because this was the man about whom Jennifer had spoken when they were down by the river. But she need only say hello and dismiss him from her mind; then dinner. . .and bed.

Peter left the room with quick strides, Geoffrey following on his heels, and the echo of voices and laughter carried through into the warm comfortable kitchen.

Then Peter was standing in the open doorway, accompanied by another man, and with the arrival of this newcomer a wind of change had entered the room, positive, forceful. . . Hadn't Jennifer said something about an aura?

He was tall, with wide shoulders sloping down to a horseman's lean waist. And his skin, bronzed from the heat that was always present up here in the far north, showed dark against hair that sprang yellow to the light. From wide-open eyes—the colour indiscernible from where she sat—his glance searched the room for his hostess.

He moved forward, his footfalls making no sound, lithe, a predator's steps, thought the watching girl. Then he was speaking. . .and Victoria didn't catch the gist of his words for a moment. All she could take in was that voice. . .

'Sevenson is bringing along a cattle-train of beef the day after tomorrow, Mrs Leith,' it was saying, 'and he's dropping me a couple of hundred head for agistment. Would you tell him as he comes through that Old Bill will let him know where I want them spread? I might not be back.'

'Yes, all right, Scott. Now, have you time to eat before you leave—to wherever it is that you're off to at this hour of the evening?' Mrs Leith was answering.

Victoria's whole body had gone rigid as that voice transported her out of the warm, brightly lit room on to a deserted railway siding. Now, glancing surreptitiously at the man she had met there, she saw teeth gleam against that tanned skin, and heard amusement in his reply. A deep, laughing amusement as he answered in that strangely soft tone, the one she remembered he had used while calling her a spoilt rich girl.

'Oh, there are always places to be off to, and all sorts of hours to start. Surely that seems to be the general idea around these parts—among all sorts of people.'

The smile Mrs Leith returned was rueful—and then it was real. An older woman's smile towards a young man she liked, thought Victoria. But her hostess was continuing, 'Yes, with you, Scott, I expect there are. It just seems a little late to be starting out visiting when you have to ride—stations and homes being so scattered.'

'They are, aren't they?' acquiesced that soft voice. 'But I expect one can always find places to visit and things to do, if one really wants to. Of course, there's always the mission. It's one of the places not too far away. . .from my home, anyhow. Also, that's one destination no one could find fault with, now could they?'

Noting that sardonic smile, wondering about him, Victoria was suddenly not wondering about obscure undercurrents as that glance swung round to settle on her.

'This is Victoria Steene, Scott,' Mrs Leith was saying. 'She's come to teach Geoffrey. Scott Courtney, Victoria. He's our nearest neighbour—from Namangilla.'

'Miss Steene!' It was surface acknowledgement only. There was no indication in those two words of greeting that he was aware of any previous meeting. Though of course he would know her. He had seen her clearly on the carriage steps—even if he didn't recognise her voice, as she had so surely done his. He just had no intention of acknowledging it. Well, he needn't think she would bring it to anyone's attention either!

So, helping Jennifer set the table, walking between it and the old-fashioned cupboards, listening to the flow of laughter and talk encircling the big room, Victoria thought how incredible were the two different personalities that this man showed.

He was laughing now while giving an emphatic no to something Geoffrey was asking of him, then turning back to Peter to answer another question.

He didn't look poor, as Jennifer had intimated. He certainly didn't act poor either. He carried about him the assurance, the almost arrogance she had already had experience of. She acknowledged that he wasn't dressed in clothes from a fashion magazine. That what he wore was almost a uniform in this day and age, the tight jeans and check shirt, except that this man wore his sleeves rolled above the elbow, showing tanned, corded muscles.

Dinner was served, and the talk was of people and places of the district, with not a word surfacing of any trip away—or any mention of an incident beside a waiting Sunlander in the middle of the night.

And later, when Jennifer called, 'Will you give me a

hand, Victoria?' she rose to take hold of cups which the younger girl was filling, and she began handing them around. As she did so, something happened that changed the whole course of the night for her.

As she leaned over to place his carefully beside their guest, he had suddenly glanced up. For the space of a hearbeat their glances held, and as she met that look the cup she was holding went down with its saucer rattling. In their depths, in the dense absolute cornflower-blue of his eyes, was an expression she couldn't read. Then, abruptly, she wasn't looking into them. They were hooded by fallen lids, and he was giving all his attention to the crisp apple pie Jennifer had set before him.

Back in her place, Victoria found she needed both hands to lift her own cup. She sat with it before her face, drinking slowly, her pie ignored. What had happened? She had certainly met more amorous glances than that unreadable one just now, and passed them off with a laugh. She had had dates, but had left them all with a shrug. She was a normal, attractive girl of almost twenty-one. But. . .not one of those partners had caused even the smallest quickening of a heartbeat.

Astringently she brought herself to task. What did she care that those eyes, and their owner, had shown no interest in her whatsoever? Showing not even the faintest suggestion, either, that they had ever met.

She told herself that she didn't know him either, and that it was just as well she had decided she was going to leave this place soon if this was the way she was going to behave.

She set down her cup, empty now, and found that her appetite had completely departed. She pushed away her dessert plate. She did see, from under downcast lashes, this neighbour from the next station glance surreptitiously at the big wall clock, and then, barely waiting to finish his pie, push back his chair. He flipped a hand in a salute to them all and departed, Peter escorting him out.

Victoria heard them laughing as their footsteps echoed over the hard veranda boards. Heard, too, a sharply ejaculated sentence echo even louder, another quick laugh, and then the thunder of hoofs galloping from the word go. It sounded to her like two horses, but with Peter returning she decided she must have been mistaken.

'What did you think of him, Victoria?' Mrs Leith was asking.

'Oh, come on, Mrs Leith!' Victoria made herself laugh carelessly as she replied. 'What should I think of someone I haven't exchanged half a dozen words with? I didn't think anything.' She told the lie barefaced.

Her employer sighed, then began to push silver this way and that about the table. She said, 'This used to be Scott's second home, but he left Namangilla when he was seventeen because of his stepmother. And the years away have changed him. He also appears to live a much more social life than seems possible up here. I only wish he'd get married and settle down.'

'Don't all mothers and older friends?' ejaculated Victoria ironically, thinking of her own mother, then added, because she wanted to know, 'Why did he leave because of his stepmother?' But she was careful to ask the question casually.

'Oh, Vivian hated living up here. She called it primitive beyond description, and when Edward, Scott's father, became ill, she moved him to the city. Then she set about stripping Namangilla. It was the scandal of the whole district.'

'But, good heavens, if it was his father's and she was his wife, wasn't she entitled?'

'No, she was not, Victoria. And I'm afraid that's the reason for this attitude of Scott's regarding some kinds of women.'

Like the kind he thinks I am, thought Victoria, enlightened.

'But he shouldn't have such ideas, Mum—he can twist most of them round his little finger,' broke in Jennifer. 'And *he* can't talk—he's always done only exactly what he wants to do. You should know that. And you should know, also, he cares for nothing and nobody—except Namangilla.'

'Except Shad,' came from Geoffrey.

'Oh, yes, and Shad, of course,' put in Peter, who had been drinking yet another cup of tea. 'He was there waiting when we went out.'

'Was he?' questioned Mrs Leith. 'I didn't hear him come.'

'Oh, come on, Aunt! You know you wouldn't hear Shad if he didn't want you to.' Sarcasm was in Peter's tone.

'But we should have heard his horse. . .and we didn't.'

'You wouldn't hear that either, if he didn't want you to.'

'Why didn't he come in with Scott, Peter?' asked Jennifer. 'He usually eats with us when Scott does.'

'How should I know? I'm not a woman, forever asking a bloke his business.'

'But where would they be off to, starting at this hour?' asked Mrs Leith again.

'Oh, Aunt!' Peter's tone held exasperation this time. 'Where would Scott be going but to meet some woman? He has enough invitations.'

'There, Mum, you should be happy that I don't want to be chasing around. That I know what I want—and who I want!' Jennifer's glance swung round to focus challengingly on Peter.

For the first time Victoria heard the placid, easygoing voice of the man leaning against a kitchen bench sharpen.

'You know I agree with your mother, Jen. All I say is that you should go out in the world a bit more, meet other people. . .'

'Rubbish, Peter! I'm not clever enough to go on at school—Mum knows that. But I can ride and muster cattle and run a station—well, nearly. And I could also run a home if things turn out the way I want them to.'

Peter only shook his head in disapproval.

Suddenly Victoria felt the walls closing in upon her. She had been travelling for three days, and then this meeting with this man. She didn't want to be drawn into Jennifer's affairs; she only wanted to get to sleep and find oblivion. She said, 'Do you think I might go to my room, Mrs Leith? I'm rather tired.'

So she left the bright kitchen and the four people behind her and walked down the dim corridor. Pressing the switch of the battery table-lamp, she closed the door and leant her back against it.

She didn't think of those newly met occupants of this place, or even of her own family. She remembered the jolt her entire body had received when she had met that glance out there; that glance from eyes so dense a blue they seemed to hold infinity within their depths.

Shaking her head, she felt the hard wood against it and abruptly decided not to try to put anything into perspective tonight. Tomorrow was another day. Tonight she would have a hot shower and go to bed—and pull the clothes right over her head.

In the bathroom between her and Jennifer's room, she stood under the streaming warmth, trying to find relaxation. Then, with a short nightdress slipped over her head, she picked up her hairbrush and walked out on to the veranda. Leaning against an upright post, she casually brushed while gazing out into the night. The stars were diamond-bright, seeming so much more brilliant than they did down south, and it was so quiet. No sound of the ordinary world noises penetrated. A breeze came suddenly wafting across from over the river—cool, pungent with the smell of eucalyptus. Oh, well, she thought, and with a shrug went inside.

In bed, burying her face into the pillow, she closed her eyes and found herself looking into the dense blue of other eyes. Restlessly she turned. She would think this whole situation out tomorrow—tonight she was going to sleep. With exhaustion and tiredness taking its toll, she did fall over the edge of the world into deep oblivion.

The next morning in the schoolroom with Geoffrey, she remembered her thoughts and decision of yesterday, but today was another day. The sky was blue, the sun shone golden—and if she didn't stay here she would most likely have to take that job in her father's office—ugh!

So she began sorting papers and setting Geoffrey to work. Then later, going through to lunch, she met the station's manager, as easygoing as his son—who was named after him—with the same hazel eyes, but with a skin wrinkled and tanned the colour of old leather.

'She's out with Peter, checking strays near Namangilla,' answered Pete Brown when asked where Jennifer was.

'Can we go after them, Mum? I've really worked hard

this morning, haven't I, Victoria?' Geoffrey threw a coaxing arm round his mother's shoulders.

'I don't know, Geoff. You've——'

'Keeping him to the grindstone all the time would defeat our purpose, Mrs Leith,' Victoria felt herself bound to interject, then added without thinking, 'We'll do some more this afternoon. . .' She broke off abruptly. Had she really decided without being aware of it that she was going to stay on up here?

'All right, if you say so, Victoria! Yes,' impatiently Mrs Leith replied to her son, 'you can go. He'll know where to find them, Pete, won't he?'

'Of course he will,' answered the manager. 'The boy knows Namangilla almost as well as he knows his own station—the result of roaming the countryside when he should have been at his lessons, no doubt. You going too?' he asked, turning to Victoria.

She shook her head. She could ride, but she didn't want to go anywhere near that place called Namangilla.

However, protests overriden, Victoria found that after a quick meal she was being escorted down to the stock-yards. She watched while a horse was cut out and saddled for her, and a trifle nervously she decided that these animals seemed a lot different from the quiet riding beasts she had been used to down south.

'Up you go,' Mr Brown told her, a hand holding the stirrup iron for her to step into.

Swinging lightly into the saddle, gingerly she patted the shining muscles beneath her. Then as a sharp smack sounded from behind, the shoulders of her mount bunched, and they were off.

This was the far north, and a tropical sun poured down heat from a sky of deep sapphire. It brought to them also the tang of gum-leaves that permeated the atmosphere all about them as the empty miles were cantered away. Then suddenly they were not empty any more, a young boy was riding at a tangent to intercept them; a loud 'cooee' echoing from him made Geoffrey turn. Slowing his headlong rush as they dropped into a walk to wait, the youngster was soon riding beside Victoria. She found herself looking into eyes that were familiar. She had seen such eyes only last night.

'This is Bobby Courtney,' Geoffrey was telling her, 'Scott's cousin. She's Miss Steene, but I call her Victoria.'

Victoria said hello—what else did one say to a small boy? Looking at him as he smiled up at her, she saw that though these eyes might be similar to those of his big cousin the expression they held was not. Still, she wanted nothing to do with either of them, the young or the old. She kicked her horse gently and it moved a little faster.

The young boy continued to ride at her side. He asked enquiringly, 'Do you help Geoff with his lessons like Scott helps me?'

'I don't know, Bobby, but I expect I do. How are you helped?'

'Oh, both Scott and Shad help me, but I don't like school work. I only want to be a jackaroo when I grow up. But Scott always says I've got to learn my lessons if I want to be a jackaroo on one of the big stations.'

'Can't you be a jackaroo on Namangilla? That's the name of your station, isn't it?'

'Oh, Namangilla doesn't belong to me. Scott owns it, and it won't run to a jackaroo for some time yet, worse luck,' said the boy.

'Why are you living up here on it, then?'

'Because I'm an orphan, and Scott looks after me.'

No sign of regret was apparent in the boy's voice or manner. However, it seemed strange, with both their names being Courtney, that this boy owned none of it, but why even wonder about it? she decided, and kicked her horse again.

So they cantered along, until almost abruptly they were surrounded by people and cattle, the bush behind them and open grassland beneath their horses' hooves.

Peter was there, and so was Jack. There was also an old man with a wrinkled, kindly face who turned out to be the Old Bill she had once heard mentioned—by a man she didn't want to remember.

'It's a pleasure to meet you, missy,' he told her. 'We like to see new faces up here.'

'We want to collect our strays before Scott's cattle-train gets here, Victoria,' explained Jennifer. 'Our stock always tries to get across to Namangilla. The grass is so much greener there.'

'And we'd better get going too,' called Peter. 'You get over there, Geoff. Move up, Jen!' His tone hurried them along.

Walking her own mount beside Geoffrey on their side of the mob, Victoria flipped a hand at Bobby's called goodbye. She also received a beaming smile and an invitation from the old man with the seamed, walnut-coloured face. 'Come and visit us, missy,' he told her, 'and I'll give you the best billy tea and damper you've ever tasted.'

He probably would, she reflected, as she smiled good-bye. She had never tasted either.

Brawling and fractious, the mob was herded towards its own land, and as her mount twisted and turned in the job for which it had been trained the sun-drenched land drifted fast into becoming the reality, her former home disappearing into the past.

She jumped, her reverie dissolving into splintered

fragments as a loud 'cooee' echoed from the other side of
the moving animals. Following Peter's intent gaze,
Victoria saw two dots that turned slowly into horsemen
riding out of the far distance. Even as she looked, they
veered sharply, the space between them closing. There
was no mistaking one of the figures who lounged so easily
in his saddle, horse and rider a part of each other.

'I thought you said you wouldn't be home, Scott,'
Peter greeted them as they came level. 'I've just finished
giving your instructions to Old Bill and Bobby. . . Hello,
Shad,' he threw to the silent form sitting so easily in the
saddle on the other side, and accepted the casually raised
hand from the dark horseman as answer enough.

He asked the fair half of the duo, 'Didn't—er—did
your rendezvous fall through?'

No laugh answered him, but those eyes glinted
wickedly like gleaming sapphires, before the lounging
form replied, 'My rendezvous, as you delicately put it,
didn't fall through. However, I did find myself with some
time to spare, so I decided to be here when the train
arrived. I need a word with Sevenson.'

From across the heaving backs of the animals,
Victoria's gaze rested on the man facing Peter. The big
slouched hat—which she remembered—was pushed to
the back of his head, corn-yellow hair showing sweat-
stained and flattened from hard riding. The horses too,
like their riders, spoke of a gruelling journey, as they
stood tired, their heads hanging.

The fair newcomer glanced around the stock spread
about; he was friendly, easy. An entirely different man
from that ruthless, menacing one she had once met and
then shut out completely from her memory. Now he was
casually walking his tired horse around the clustered mob
of beasts, and abruptly her own mount sidled sharply,

taking note of her hands tightening unexpectedly on the reins.

Scott Courtney was coming her way. Victoria straightened her relaxed position and came quickly upright—but he was only inspecting the cattle. Then he wasn't just inspecting stock; he had turned, facing her. His back to the others, he pulled off his hat for the briefest second as if greeting her.

Her face hard, all expression willed out of it, Victoria returned his look. He was certainly no man about town today, his clothes showing the strain of hard usage. His tanned sun-glazed skin still held the smoothness she had noticed last night, but now showed golden as the sunshine struck at it—he had not shaved this morning.

However, it was his eyes that she made herself meet; those blue eyes that were gazing directly into her own. Then suddenly amusement flashed into them, creating dancing pinpoints as he took in the hostility of her glance.

'Not taking any midnight walks around here by yourself, I hope, Miss Steene?'

Oh, so he did remember her, she thought acidly. She replied through clenched white teeth, 'No, I'm not. But then I'm not stranded in a stationary train waiting for heaven knows what. . .'

He laughed, his body shaking silently, she noticed wrathfully. Anyone looking from across the moving cattle backs would imagine he was just being polite to a visitor to the north. Then he was speaking again, but so quietly that the words would be inaudible to anyone else above the movement of horses, the lowing of the animals, the creak of leather as the other riders and cattle-dogs kept the mob in order.

'You might not be stranded in a waiting train. But with your propensity to go strolling at all hours, with your ideas that you can do what you like, whenever you like—weren't those the words you used?—you could cause a lot of trouble for a lot of people.'

'Well, don't think you'll be one of the people I could cause trouble for, Mr Courtney. Just keep out of my way. Because I intend to keep completely out of yours.'

'Oh, I'll be doing that. Still, I don't want to be called away from the running of my station to join a search-party lookng for you, that's all! So kindly take a word of warning.'

'I really don't need warnings from you. I'm not stupid, whatever you might think. Also,' she shot a hostile glance at the figure lounging there so casually on his mount, 'whatever your impression is of me, I wouldn't like to tell you mine of you!'

Without giving him a chance to reply, she had kicked at her mount, and without looking almost bumped into the dark horseman who had also circled the cattle and was riding to join them.

He smiled, a hand half raised in greeting, and she was brushing past with just a short word, furious with the man she had left laughing behind her, when she stopped. What would this man think of her behaviour—this part-aborigine?

So she smiled at him, and when Victoria extended her natural warm smile her whole face lighted up and she was beautiful. She said, 'Hello. I'm Victoria.'

He answered slowly, pleasantly, 'Yes, I know. I'm called Shad.'

Victoria was suddenly laughing and told him, 'Yes, I know.'

He was not ebony-black like Jack. This face showed the colour of chocolate, and his hair under the pushed-back big hat showed flattened and damp from hard riding also. His hand went up in a half-wave and he was moving after his companion, and soon they were disappearing in a fast, loping canter.

Victoria found her attention called away from the two vanishing riders. The mob was being urged on, with Geoff and Peter yip-yipping along its flank, with the dogs urging strays back where they belonged, with the riders and their mounts keeping the animals in a close compact herd.

CHAPTER THREE

THE sun continued to pour down its molten heat, the cattle to bellow, and as her horse twisted and turned Victoria thought of the men who had just left them. The kindness which had seemed to flow from the dark one, the ruthlessness and arrogance from the other.

Thinking of that ruthlessness and arrogance, she wondered suddenly what Scott Courtney had been doing a thousand miles or so from this, his home ground. Oh, well, it was probably connected with some woman, as Jennifer had intimated—and it was none of her business. All she was interested in now was a long cool bath.

Later, with hair washed and set in the big old-fashioned rollers which Mrs Leith had dug out for her because her electric blow-drier couldn't be just plugged in and switched on here, Victoria lay back in a big canvas chair, allowing the sun to dry it.

Eyes closed against the golden light, a form floated before the shut lids. Sweat-stained, dust-ingrained, clothes crumpled from long hours in the saddle—how was it possible for such an image to present that air of assurance, that atmosphere of almost arrogance?

Yet that *was* the element which had coloured the space around him. And Victoria's lips thinned as she remembered the silent laughter which had shaken him after he had spoken with her. Apparently he also thought he could say and do what he liked to anyone he liked.

OK, she thought coldly, this was a vast land, and thank goodness there would be no way they could accidentally bump into one another. And she would make it her business to see that she wouldn't be in his vicinity any other way. But good resolutions had a habit of going astray—as this one did. Not five minutes later.

She almost jumped when a loud voice called from the room behind her. 'We're going across to Namangilla. . . Jennifer, Victoria. Sevenson's coming through and Pete says he wants to see the stock. Talk about Scott's personal smoke-signals! He's supposed not to be here, but when his cattle arrive early there he is! So if you two are coming you'd better come now, because we're leaving.'

I'd like to go. I've never seen a cattle-train, thought Victoria. But hadn't she just resolved that she would keep away from any vicinity which might hold that man whose attitude sent her blood pressure up to boiling-point?

'Are you going, Jen?' she called to the other occupant of the veranda, who was leaning on the railing as she gazed out over the river.

'Yes, I guess so, I. . .'

An engine started up a short distance away and was gunned into a roar. The younger girl turned to run, so Victoria, rising quickly, ran too.

They squeezed in beside Geoffrey in the back, and it was only as they were bouncing along a potholed track that Victoria realised her hair was still in rollers. Her hands went up and she began discarding the plastic gadgets on to the seat beside her.

'As I haven't got a comb, it's just as well I don't care,' she muttered to herself, combing with her fingers until her hair hung, a shining, tumbling mass about her face and neck.

Travelling on what seemed only a hint of a road, Victoria wondered how on earth their driver kept on it. . .and drove so quickly too, because the countryside outside was flying past. No one seemed worried, so this was the way they must always drive.

'How far is Namangilla?' she asked.

'Quite close, as distance goes in the outback.' It was Uncle Pete who answered. 'I imagine that in the beginning both homesteads were built close to the boundary line for companionship's sake. But we're not going to the house now, we're going to one of the billabongs, because that's where Sevenson will unload his train.'

'Billabongs? Goodness!' Victoria started to laugh. 'You know, I could almost be back at primary school, learning about such things.'

'Up here, they are a fact of life, and anyone lucky enough to possess any gives thanks. However, these billabongs aren't the natural phenomenon. Old man Courtney built them in all along his small tributary, giving much more water to the land than it would normally have. That's why Namangilla's one of the top properties in the far north.

'We'll have to take you to visit the big dam down at the far end while you're up here,' he was continuing. 'It's a local beauty spot and a famous picnicking place; and Scott sees to it that it remains that way.' Uncle Pete stopped speaking, concentrating upon his driving.

It took only a few more minutes before a stain of dust began to form on their horizon, and then, coming on the breeze to them, the reason for it.

Pouring down ramps from the enormous lorry train was a brawling, struggling mass of cattle, jumping sideways, on top of one another, underneath one another. . .all ways. However, once free and on solid ground again they just stood, waiting.

Peter was there, his cut-out pony twisting and turning,

sharing the scene with Bobby and Old Bill. Two strange men on foot were among the animals trying to keep the ramp ends clear. But the owner of all this turmoil wasn't in evidence.

Pulling the Land Rover to a stop some distance away from the busy scene, Uncle Pete stepped out, and like a quicksilver eel Geoffrey was following. He was grabbed by his mother. 'Oh, no, you don't, my boy! You're not going over there on foot,' she informed him sharply.

'But, Mum—oh, all right,' and because he had no option he too just stood and watched from a distance.

Slowly order was taking place out of chaos, stock being moved away by the horsemen, tired, dispirited, unbelievably thin. Victoria gazed at them with pity. Mrs Leith, catching her glance, told her briskly,

'There's no need to be sorry for them, Victoria. They're on Namangilla now. Scott will have them in show condition in no time.'

As if the mention of his name had conjured him up, the station's owner made an appearance. He spoke to one of the men, and then the huge juggernaut was backing and turning, disappearing into the gathering dusk.

'You'll have to be careful you don't lose any of these, Scott,' Victoria heard Uncle Pete say. 'They're in poor condition.'

'They won't be when I've finished with them, though,' she also heard the soft reply.

Bobby rode over, greeting Victoria as if she were a long-lost friend, and from the corner of her vision she saw a yellow head swing round, and was aware of a long assessing look raking her.

She felt burning colour sweep from breast to neck to cheeks, and was violently angry with herself. No one had ever made her blush like this. And this man, this ignorant man, was not going to make it happen again, she decided furiously.

Why did he take this attitude towards her? she wondered. She knew, as she had known absolutely last night at the dinner table, that whatever the stories were about this man and his women interest in her wasn't the name of his game.

'You'll come, won't you, Victoria?' Bobby was urging.

Before she could reply, Jennifer was doing it for her. 'You'll have to ask Mother. I don't know if we'll be able to.'

'Ask me what?' Mrs Leith turned away from Pete to ask.

'They're having a picnic on Sunday and have invited us. The swimming-pool is beaut now, Bobby says.' Geoffrey put his bit in coaxingly, his arm around his mother's shoulders. He was adding, 'You know we can't swim in our river just now, Mum—it's too low. Can't we go, please?'

For a moment his mother didn't reply, then a new voice broke in. 'The mission crowd is coming over, Mrs Leith, so why don't you all come and we'll make a family picnic of it?' Mocking, satirical, unbelievably aware, the words fell silken among the small group.

Beside Victoria, Jennifer's glance went to Peter, then on to her mother. 'Oh, come on, Mum! Of course we should go! Up here, we need to see one another when we can.'

She was perfectly right, Victoria knew, but she suspected that that wasn't her reason.

However, Scott's figure, dust-begrimed, hat pushed completely off the lemon-yellow hair now as the shadows lengthened, presented only a perfectly grave countenance to the party standing by the Land Rover. His eyes

weren't grave, though, Victoria knew, seeing those dancing pinpoints of laughter in the cornflower-blue depths.
She had seen that manifestation before. Then, too, he
had been sitting indolently on a horse. Now he threw a
leg over the pommel of his saddle, as if to make himself
comfortable while awaiting their answer.

'OK, Scott, I'll be in that.' Peter's interjection came
after Jennifer had sent another imploring glance at him.
Then he turned from her with a shrug and added with a
smile curling his lips, 'Seeing it's holiday-time, mate,
with probably lots of extra help on tap, it's about time
you shared the good things of life with us all.'

Scott laughed, no mockery there for Peter. His horse
sidled, and, gentling it, he said, 'I do believe there's extra
help on tap there—however, whether it will benefit you
or not, I wouldn't like to say.'

Jennifer asked, 'When was this picnic arranged, Scott?
I think it's a great idea.'

'Do you, now, Jen? I had the idea you might be
considered too young for my picnics.' There was no
doubt about the mockery in these words, and then
abruptly he had turned, saying, 'What about you, Miss
Steene? Do you think you might be considered too young
for this kind of junketing too?'

Victoria glanced across the few yards separating them.
Glanced at a man who had no right to carry that assured
air of arrogance as he sat there, clad in old clothes, dust-
covered, with perspiration-streaked features.

She replied—and, like this morning, the words came
through white clenched teeth—'I wouldn't know, Mr
Courtney. People from the mission sound innocuous
enough. However, possibly there might be others there
that my parents could think unsuitable for me to mix
with!'

'Victoria!' The scandalised interjection came from Mrs Leith.

Bobby was glancing back and forth among the grown-ups, a puzzled expression between his brows, aware with a child's sure knowledge that something was wrong, while not knowing what.

Peter exclaimed, 'Oh, my word!'

Old Bill had edged his horse back a few yards and was watching the tableau with shrewd old eyes.

Geoffrey, in his brash way, had begun to speak, but his mother's suddenly tight grip on his arm stopped the words in mid-sentence.

Uncle Pete, in the act of stepping into the cabin of the Land Rover, turned, a wide grin splitting his face in two as he said, 'It's about time someone gave you your come-uppance, Scott!'

But the intense blue eyes opposite showed no chagrin, no discomfiture. They were dancing with laughter, and against that bronzed dusty face they showed up like deep sapphires.

All he answered in that deceptively soft voice of his was, 'In that case you'd better get Mrs Leith to vet them—if she decides to come herself, that is.'

Oh, I hate him! And why did I ever have to meet him? reflected Victoria furiously. She had thought her words—her very rude words—would disconcert him; that they were unanswerable.

But that hateful voice had had the last word. Having to get her employer to vet her outings, indeed!

I won't go to his rotten picnic, she decided flatly, and turning away came to a halt as the sky above was filled with a cloud of vivid carnation-pink—galahs wending their way homewards for the night. She looked up as they all were doing at, for that brief moment, something which was exquisite, beautiful.

'They are lovely, seen in the mass like this,' said Mrs Leith.

'Yes, they are,' replied Scott, but only absently. Then he was giving that casual half-wave which seemed to take the place of more formal leavetaking up here, and had turned to go.

As they left themselves, a glance behind showed Victoria three horsemen, one old, one young, and one very young, loping easily along side by side. Then suddenly a lingering sunray piercing horizontally between the trees caught for the briefest moment a dazzling gleam of gold. That head was uncovered this time.

'You don't like him, Victoria?'

Startled, bringing her gaze back from a sunset that was staining the edge of the world with the vividness of scarlet and crimson, Victoria wondered what to answer.

'Oh, I wouldn't say that, Mrs Leith,' she replied, smiling at the face turned to her from the front seat. 'He just rubs me up the wrong way, that's all.'

'He's had reason to dislike city women of a certain kind, Victoria. . .' Her employer's words trailed off as a violent streak of lightning bathed them all in a zigzag of brilliance.

'He might have had that reason once upon a time, when his stepmother took everything that wasn't nailed down—and a lot of things that were—but he hasn't now,' interjected Uncle Pete when the rumble of thunder had passed over them. 'Now, he's sitting pretty, on top of the world. He'll have Namangilla as much a showplace as the Hamilton run before he's finished.'

'But Jen said he was poor,' returned Victoria uncertainly.

Their driver laughed, and went on laughing. 'That's funny!' he said when he had paused for breath, then added, 'I expect he might have to go to the bank for some ready cash occasionally, but any big pastoral company would jump at buying Namangilla—if they could only get hold of it—for around ten or fifteen million dollars, give or take a few dollars in between.'

Victoria gasped. She herself came from a comfortable home, but millions. . .that was another story altogether. 'You're joking, aren't you, Uncle Pete?' she asked uncertainly.

'I never joke about that sort of money, my girl,' he said, then as another zigzag of lightning criss-crossed the darkening sky he added, 'Better put up the windows. Here it comes!'

So that was why Scott Courtney carried that air of complete assurance, of almost arrogance—even when sitting carelessly on a tired dispirited horse, thought Victoria acidly.

Speeding homewards, the streaming much-needed rain pouring against the windows, Victoria made herself ask, 'But why was it wrong for his stepmother to take what was surely her husband's property?'

'Yes, it *was* her husband's property, but Vivian went the wrong way about things. She and Scott were always polite, but politeness was all that it was; they didn't like one another. And for my sins I was stuck out there on the veranda when the blow-up came.' Uncle Pete stopped talking for a moment to switch on the Land Rover's spotlight to look at an animal beside the track.

Apparently satisfied, he resumed speaking, and Victoria gave all her attention to the words coming over the front seat towards her; she didn't want to miss any.

Whatever she thought of Scott Courtney, she wanted to hear all that was said about him.

'I was there because Edward had been taken sick at our place, and I'd ridden over to see how he was. I was going up the back steps and heard their voices, and didn't know whether to leave and make a noise, or stay and keep quiet. Vivian's voice echoed sharply, while Scott's. . . Well, you know how he gets when he's angry.'

'Yes, soft like silk, which makes you feel cold,' interjected Jennifer.

'"You can't sell that herd," I heard Scott say. "It's not the time for it." Vivian replied, "I *am* selling it, Scott. Look, your father's ill, and this sickness is going to go on for a long time. I would like us to talk sensibly. I'll see that you get your share. I don't want to deprive you . . ." Here, Scott interrupted even more softly as he asked, "My share of what, Vivian?" "I'm selling Namangilla, Scott. I've had an agent check into it, and we'll get a lot of money, a very great deal of money, so you'll be a well-off young man and can buy into anything. . ." "Does my father know of these plans, Vivian?" These words came out to me so softly I could hardly hear them.' Uncle Pete shook his head and said, 'I also knew then that I should have left, but I couldn't make myself move.'

I wouldn't have been able to either, if I'd been in your place, thought Victoria.

'However, Vivian was answering by then, saying, "No, I don't want him bothered. He knows I only want what's best for him, to allow him to have the best doctors and nursing later on." "Well, I've got news for you, Vivian," that voice like tearing silk answered, "And that news is that you're not selling Namangilla—Namangilla's mine! Also, Dad can stay up here for quite some time yet. I know! I've also checked!"

'"Your father is *not* staying here. He's coming to the city with me. I'm not staying in this place for a day longer than I have to." Vivian was shouting by this time. You must realise, Victoria, that she wasn't bad, she did love Edward, but she was stupid! Things could have been worked out differently, and all these bitter years avoided.

'When he spoke again, Scott's voice had lost its softness, and I wouldn't have liked that tone to be used to me. Swinging round, he said over a shoulder, "I'm going. And not back to school! And also I'm not going to be a well-off young man either. And you," he laughed back at her, such a laugh, "can just *try* selling Namangilla."'

'What happened then, Uncle Pete?' asked Victoria urgently, because they were home, and Mrs Leith was worrying about windows being left open, Scott Courtney and his affairs disappearing from her mind.

But Victoria wanted very much to know why Namangilla hadn't been sold. Because with that arrogant man living there and still apparently owning it, it could not have been. She also wanted to know why it had been allowed to go to rack and ruin as Jennifer had said.

So she said again quickly, 'Why wasn't it sold, then, Uncle Pete?'

'Oh, because of some fool idea of the man from England who bought it over a century ago. The deeds were left in trust for any Courtney heir; but that damned Scott was lucky. He was informed just six months ago that the trust was for a hundred years and is now being wound up. Look,' he was saying as he turned away, Scott Courtney and his affairs obviously dismissed from his mind also, 'I'm off,' and he was. Only the echo of a departing Land Rover returned in his place.

Mrs Leith was busy mopping up water and muttering about a meal to be prepared. So Victoria collected Geoffrey and marched him to the schoolroom for an hour's work.

CHAPTER FOUR

'VICTORIA!'

'Yes, Mrs Leith?'

'We're going along to the mission. Better change into jeans,' the older woman added, taking in the thin, low-necked cotton dress and the bare-legged sandalled feet. 'We'll probably be gone the whole day and get home after dark.'

As she turned to leave, Victoria threw out a restraining hand. 'Couldn't I stay home, please, Mrs Leith? I do have work to prepare. I really don't feel like going all that way today when I'll be meeting them all on Sunday.'

'But you'll be on your own; you won't like that!'

Victoria laughed. 'For a few hours? Of course I will. I've got a new book I've been waiting to read. . .'

'Very well, if you're sure, then. Look, Pete will be here in a minute, so I'd better be off. Geoffrey and Jen are already out there waiting.' For a moment longer the older woman stood irresolutely in the doorway, then, shrugging, said, 'There's no chance of anyone turning up here to molest you, but I'll tell Pete to leave one of the dogs free just the same. Oh—don't go down to the river, will you?'

'No, I won't.' Victoria was only too happy to concede this, and following her employer outside to see them off she noticed that it was the Jaguar, not the more familiar Land Rover, that was waiting.

She stood leaning against the veranda railing, listening to the fast disappearing sound of the engine until only

silence came back to her. Above, leaves on a eucalyptus
gum shivered in a gentle breeze, and from a sky as deeply
blue as pure lapis lazuli the sun poured down its warmth
over a wide, empty universe.

'Seeing I used work as an excuse to remain here at
home, I expect I'd better get back to the grindstone,' she
murmured to herself, then added, 'Geoffrey might be off
playing the wag, but he's sure going to make up for this
stolen day. So first I'll prepare his lessons, then afterwards I'll take my lunch outside to enjoy with my new
book.'

It was just before noon when she sent her chair
skittering back over the polished lino, and, rising,
stretched hugely. Making her way to the kitchen, she
siphoned warm water from the side-tank on the big
combustion stove and placed it in the centre to boil.

'I think a dagwood sandwich suits this occasion,' she
muttered. 'If I'm going to read, I'll need a hand free to
turn pages.' She worked swiftly, then before turning to
the stove to make her tea gazed at her big sandwich with
satisfaction. Then, just as suddenly, she swung round
with that look wiped completely from her face.

A step had sounded on the hard boards of the veranda,
and with a hand still holding the boiling kettle she turned
to stare a trifle apprehensively at the wide-open doorway.
No one should be coming here. Then from the corner of
her eye a movement caught her attention. The big cattle-
dog was slinking along, crouched low down—but even
as she looked it was upright again, turning unconcernedly
away.

A breath of relief escaped her. Peter, probably returning home early for some lunch, she thought—and
stopped her hand making the tea. She might need a
bigger pot.

It was just as well she did hold only an empty container, for suddenly nerveless fingers had allowed it to slip. Because standing in the doorway, a hand raised to knock, was Scott Courtney—bare-headed, the big hat hanging free from leather thongs.

Victoria remained rooted where she stood, unable to make herself move or speak, her breath caught. Across a silent room their glances met and held. The hand which had been raised to knock fell to his side, and as if that small movement had broken a spell, slowly, carefully Victoria retrieved the teapot.

She heard herself say, and the words sounded laboured, 'The family is not at home, Mr Courtney.'

He walked a few steps to pause just inside the doorway. 'I've just come from Pete's house. I wanted to see either him or Peter. You wouldn't know where they are, by any chance?'

Today there was no mockery. . .no menace either. He was only an ordinary caller wanting to know the where-abouts of someone. But no, she corrected herself, he would never be an ordinary caller. That aura, that force she had felt when he had first walked into this room the night of her arrival, was still there. She felt it reaching out to her.

Abruptly she took hold of herself. *She* might feel it, but *he* received no emanation from her. His face expressionless, those extraordinary eyes hooded, he stood waiting for her answer.

Taking a deep breath, she managed to reply casually. 'They've gone to the mission—Uncle Pete wanted to see the doctor if he's there. I think Peter's working some-where near your own boundary.'

'OK, thanks. . . You might just tell Pete I was looking for him.' Again came that gesture she was beginning to become familiar with up here, as with a hand half raised in farewell he turned to leave.

What made her say it, she could never afterwards decide. The words came without volition. 'Would you like some lunch. . .or a cup of tea? I was just making some.'

The yellow head swung back over a shoulder, then the whole lissom body followed it. The mouth didn't answer; those cornflower-blue eyes looked her over from head to toe. She was almost beginning to say, forget it, I'm sorry I asked, when the reply came.

'Yes, thank you, I would like some lunch.'

She almost gaped at him. She couldn't believe she was hearing those polite words and that tone from this man.

'Yes. . .all right. . .' She stopped herself stuttering, and resumed. 'I'm only having a sandwich, but there's heaps of food in the fridge. Would you prefer cold meat and a salad?'

The visitor's glance had swung round to the concoction she had just finished making, and he said, 'What about that?'

She felt her cheeks colour, and told him, 'Oh, that's a dagwood—a double-decker sandwich. My sister and I often make them if we're on our own.'

'OK, I'd like one of those, please.'

For a moment she stood looking helplessly across the room at him, then shrugged and began to cut bread. Then because it was the way she had been brought up she tried to make polite conversation, but the man didn't help, she thought indignantly. He just lounged indolently against the wall by the doorway, silent.

'We used not to have meat, my sister and I. Only tons of salad and pickles and suchlike,' she tried again, the silence making her nervous. 'But the meat is always so good up here that I frequently add it,' she indicated the cold roast from which she was slicing.

'Yes, this is meat country.' He must have decided to answer her.

She gazed at her finished work and wondered what he would think of it. Her glance swung sideways and saw that his look was fixed on the enormous sandwich. She turned her eyes sharply away. Placing it beside her own on a tray already prepared, she turned to make the tea for a second time—then paused once again. Abruptly a thought had surfaced.

'Is Shad with you, or anywhere near?' she asked, remembering suddenly that someone had once said that where Scott was, Shad wouldn't be far away.

The eyes across from her were unexpectedly wide open. Scott said, 'Why? Are you worrying about having to invite him to lunch as well?'

Puzzled by that tone which had so suddenly changed from politeness to the bleak, cold one which she remembered from the railway siding episode, she began to answer, 'Oh, no, there's plenty of food. I was only. . .' Abruptly she broke off, and when she resumed speaking, it was her tone that carried astringency as the meaning of his cold enquiry hit at her.

'Oh, no,' she said crisply, 'I wasn't worrying about having to invite Shad to lunch. If I had to choose between you two with whom I'd rather share my meal, I'll be very happy to tell you my choice!'

Heavens, was he never the same man twice? she wondered. His face had lost that closed, ruthless look it had so unexpectedly taken on, and the smile he sent her now was friendly. He had never before looked at her like that; she couldn't believe it. He levered himself away from the wall, and taking the kettle from her poured the boiling water.

Victoria placed the pot upon the tray, and naturally, automatically, indicated for him to carry it. And just as automatically the man from Namangilla lifted it and said, 'You don't eat in the kitchen? Do you want it carried through to the dining-room?'

'When there's an outside filled with sunshine and trees to sit beneath, of course I don't,' she replied, and brushed past him to the open door.

Down the veranda, across a few yards of hard-beaten earth, she walked to the strip of lawn under a large shady tree. She sank down on one of the white metal chairs. Scott placed the tray on the table before her.

She handed over his napkin-covered sandwich, then taking up the big teapot poised both it and a jug of milk over one of the cups. 'Milk?' a raised eyebrow asked.

'No milk. Two sugars, please.'

Pouring, Victoria remarked casually, 'That's unusual. Mostly in these diet-conscious days it's the other way around.'

'When you live and work a great deal in the outside, as Shad and I used to do, you find it more convenient to carry sugar,' he answered, then added, 'I wouldn't have thought, however, that you had any need to worry about dieting.' He sat back and watched her pour her own tea with milk and no sugar.

Feeling the colour rising to her cheeks, Victoria was furious with herself. She had had much more personal remarks addressed to her, and had returned them in kind with little or no effort. But with this man——! She answered coldly, '*I* wasn't being personal! *I* was just making conversation.'

'But I was personal. I always speak the truth!'

Was there a hidden meaning in those words? What was the nuance that coloured them? She didn't know, and she wasn't going to worry about it. She turned a shoulder to him, and reached for her dagwood. Taking a bite from the corner of the piled-up sandwich, she didn't care how she looked while doing it. She would also have to start learning not to care what this man said or did.

The sky above was a burning turquoise arch, the shade hemming them in, thick and cool. A gentle breeze from across the river wafted its scent of eucalyptus all about them. Everything was fine. She would just get on with her lunch and let that man beside her get on with his.

So, eating slowly, she kept her gaze from her guest, fixing it on the trellis of bougainvillaea that protected this small piece of garden. And that was no hardship. She loved to look at it, to lose her senses in its vivid beauty of royal purple.

She nearly jumped when Scott said, 'I've never tasted anything better than these things. What was it you called them?'

Amazed, she turned to face him. He grinned, saying, 'Why that incredulous look? Is it because you think that only bully-beef and damper are my normal fare——?'

'I don't think anything of the kind,' Victoria interrupted sharply. 'Even if I know what bully-beef is, which I do, or damper, which I don't, what you normally eat is none of my business. But dagwoods are concoctions which only some people like. My father would be horrified if one was served up to him.'

'You mentioned a father and a sister. Is that your family?' he asked.

'Oh, no!' Victoria's face lit up. 'I have a mother and a brother too. But we don't have a lot to do with our father. He's always very busy and we're not allowed to worry him. He's a surgeon. What about you?' Speaking of her family, she had forgotten her previous encounters with this man, and she turned to him, smiling. 'I've gathered your parents are gone and that you don't have any brothers or sisters. But besides Bobby, is there. . .?'

Oh, lord, there he goes again! she thought crossly, as his face took on that familiar arrogant look.

'Don't tell me you haven't heard the story of my life! From the beginning to the end. . .including all the juicy bits in between!' he said.

'No, I haven't heard the story of your life,' began Victoria angrily. 'Something has been said, yes—something about some family trouble, but that's all. Oh, I did have a warning from Jennifer advising me that it would be unwise to get interested in you; that you already had more than your share of female companions. It was quite unnecessary, believe me. . .

'However, Uncle Pete mentioned, when we were driving back from seeing those poor cattle delivered, that your property puts you in the millionaire class. Perhaps that's why you think you can speak how you like to the ordinary common people!' Again she was furious with him. He was shaking with that sudden, silent laughter she had noticed before.

'Namangilla,' he said then, 'is worth a lot of money. And yes, there was some family trouble, and I did leave it when I was young. However, now. . .'

Beside her, he shifted as if making a move to rise and go. Victoria said quickly, 'But you have Bobby. I know about him, because he told me himself.'

'Oh, yes.' A smile she hadn't seen before chased itself across his face. 'Oh, yes,' he repeated, 'I certainly have Bobby. Though actually he's only a cousin two or three times removed. But yes, I do have a cousin!'

There was no thought of denying young Bobby, and Victoria said, 'Is he really only a distant cousin? I imagined that with his eyes so exactly like your own, he. . .' She broke off sharply. Oh, hell, what a stupid, stupid thing to let her unruly mouth say! She sat waiting in confusion for him to turn his mocking smile on her.

However, no laughter lit up his face or coloured those eyes with dancing lights. They remained obscure, hidden by fallen lids. When he did speak her held-in breath was slowly allowed to escape. 'Yes, we do have the same sort of eyes. It's a family trait.' He moved to send a glance through those same eyes in the direction of the sun. He said, 'I've got work to do, I'd better be on my way. Thank you for the lunch. I enjoyed it.'

Victoria, also on her feet, threw out a dismissing hand to his thanks. She said quickly, 'I expect you have to check upon those poor animals that arrived the other day?'

'No. They're coming along very nicely.' Then, and somehow she thought the words were uttered with deliberate intent, he continued, 'No, I have another affair that I have to see to,' and Victoria saw, suddenly, unexpectedly, that wicked, dancing laughter which came to colour those eyes into glinting sapphire.

She met that intense blue gaze and abruptly relaxed. It was nothing to do with her; he was amused at something. . .some idea that he had in the pipeline. But, smiling happily across at him, she found that out of the blue she was being held immobile at one end of a strong invisible cord stretching tightly between them. Tension was there, and a desire she had never felt before. She shivered, and half reached out a hand for him to take. . .then allowed it to fall. This was Scott, whom

Jennifer had told her not to get involved with. . .who had more than his share of women.

Suddenly, however, he was smiling fully at her, and she felt her heart jolt. Then, swinging on his heels, he was saying over his shoulder, 'I'll see you on Sunday?'

'Yes,' was all she could find to answer. But she knew definitely that she *would* be going to his picnic. She watched him walk away with that same lithe jungle tread she had already noted. Then came the swift clip-clop of hooves walking, then a faster clippety-clop as horse and rider went into a loping canter.

Her gaze went out across the river, taking in without noticing a horizon lost in heat-haze. She knew she had to get this last hour into perspective. She was thinking far too much of a man she had met so few times—and they had not been friendly times either. A man who had not even touched her—except in anger while helping her into a darkened railway carriage.

Still, he had eaten his lunch with her. And, being Scott, he would have walked away if it had pleased him to do so. Then her heart lurched as she remembered that heart-breaking smile he had given her as he turned to leave, and, suddenly boneless, her body slipped down into the chair behind. And later, as she tried to read, no printed words penetrated her consciousness. There was only Scott Courtney's face looking up at her from every page.

Finally she closed her book, rose and, gathering up her tray, found suddenly she was folding with careful fingers the napkin Scott had used. Realisation of what she was absently doing brought her back to sanity. How stupid could she be? She took up the tray and marched swiftly inside.

CHAPTER FIVE

VICTORIA turned over restlessly, aware in a consciousness beyond her that she was dreaming. She didn't want to dream about a face that showed dark bronze beneath citrine-yellow hair. She pushed a hand up against the brightness of it. . .and came suddenly awake. Dazzling sunlight was all about her, a wide-open window framing swaying branches against an early morning turquoise sky.

Of course. Today was Sunday, and she knew what that day was bringing. She pushed aside the mosquito net, showered, then made her way out to the kitchen. Taking up a bowl of paw-paw and passion-fruit, she settled herself on one side of the big kitchen table.

'Isn't it a blessing that tropical fruit grows so well up here, Mrs Leith?' she remarked absently. 'We have to pay the earth for it at home.'

'Yes, thank goodness, it's a good stand-by, because we have so many kinds, and it can be used for umpteen things.'

'Yes,' agreed Victoria, but replying only absently. Although she loved all these fruits, just now they weren't what she was interested in. She asked the question she had been preparing all morning. 'Who is Shad, Mrs Leith? I mean, in what relation to Scott?'

'Oh, Shad. He's part-aborigine.' Mrs Leith finished squeezing oranges before continuing slowly, 'Scott's mother was ill for a long time after he was born, so Shad was brought into the house to keep her own little son company. He was the son of Namangilla's European

55

foreman and the same age as Scott. They're practically
brothers, Victoria, and left Namangilla together when
both of them were seventeen to work one of the Hamilton
stations. They're back now, thank goodness, so things
are all right again.'

She added as if their conversation had brought something to mind, 'You'll have to go and see the Namangilla
homestead one day. It's an old colonial and quite a period
piece.'

No, she wouldn't, thought Victoria as she went to the
sink to run her plate under the tap, unless. . . But she
was glad she had asked and found out about Shad.

Later, in her corner of the big Jaguar that Peter was
sending swiftly along the potholed road, she wondered
what sort of a Scott she was going to meet. The cold,
contemptuous stranger she had first met, the hard-riding
dusty cavalier, sitting so indolently on a tired, dispirited
horse, laughing at her. Or the man she had shared lunch
with; the man from whom had stretched a line of
electricity which had encircled her whole body in static.
Even now, remembering, she felt the same tingling shock
wash over her.

She turned her face sharply to shelter it from other
eyes, then deliberately slowing her breath told herself not
to be stupid; that she would have been better off if she
had followed her initial decision to leave this outback
land.

The big car was slowing, then pulling to a stop.
Victoria heard an exclamation from Jennifer as they
stepped out. 'Oh, look who's here, Mum!'

At that tone, at those words, Victoria followed her
companion's pointing hand, and saw a woman emerge
from a cluster of cars to join a man standing close by.

They stood, sunlight striking glints from hair that was

jet-black and golden yellow. Two pieces of coloured cotton showed that the woman had a figure which had been born for a bikini. Victoria felt an entirely natural pang of envy as she took in that sculptured body topped with its glamorous raven's-wing hair.

'Have you come up to the back of beyond to visit your father, Joanna?' Unusual sweetness was in Jennifer's tone as she greeted the feminine half of the couple strolling in their direction, then she added, 'This is Victoria Steene— Joanna Chiltern, Victoria.'

'Yes, I'm going to help Dad for a week or so, until our final results come out,' replied this girl who had just nodded a careless hello to Victoria. She was adding, 'And of course besides other attractions which might also be on offer up here,' an upward seductive glance went to the man standing beside her, 'working in a tropical clinic with Dad will help my career later.'

Oh, so she was a doctor, this woman who was smiling so warmly at her companion. He only replied easily, shaking his head, 'You're too beautiful for your own good, Joanna, but keep your cotton-picking hands off me. Because I'm certainly not one of those attractions on offer up here. I'm just a working man out on the farm.'

Joanna laughed delightedly, then her hand curled possessively round his arm as she answered, 'We'll have to see, then, what propinquity comes up with, won't we?'

'Oh, yes, we can always see,' came the smiling rejoinder. But, listening carefully, Victoria thought that his tone held a curious nuance. Scott's lips were still smiling, but his eyes weren't. They were half shut, as if against the sun. But she knew better. She had seen him use that mannerism before, on another special occasion.

They moved off, leaving in their wake a trail of laughter and greetings. Victoria also found herself involved in greetings, from all sorts of people. Then she stood watching as Jennifer put her hand on Peter's arm just as possessively as another girl had done to another man.

Then, turning to glance about her, Victoria thought Uncle Pete had been right about this place as a picnic spot. Situated on a bend of the river, calm, shallow water reflecting the trailing branches overhanging its surface, it was a fantastic site for such a gathering, and brightly coloured holiday clothes scattered over emerald-green shorn grass was only another decoration.

Her mind caught up in this last impression, Victoria suddenly sent her glance swinging after that strolling couple, realising abruptly that the few times she had met Scott she had had no idea at all what sort of clothes he had been wearing—except that they had left a memory of hard work.

Her lips curled into a smile as she thought he could well have had nothing on, for all she would have noticed the very first time they had met. All her memory retained was a contemptuous voice and a silent predator's jungle tread as he hurried her to the steps of her compartment.

This time she glanced fully at him as he stood laughing now with two elderly ladies. He was wearing white shorts with a black motif on the left leg coupled with a white silk shirt carrying the same design on the breast pocket. These were not clothes bought off the rack. They were designer creations. They were the kind her brother bought and wore. Everything about Scott Courtney seemed to be contradictory, she decided as she gazed at him across the swirl of moving people.

The yellow head swung suddenly around, and even with such a distance separating them Victoria felt the pull of that invisible line that once again stretched between them. For only a moment in time, but for what seemed an aeon to her, that gaze held. Then she was turning sharply away to pick up her camera. Taking snaps was a valid excuse to be by herself for a minute or so, and she needed time to get a jumping pulse and shaking legs into order. So in her short green shorts and paler jade shirt she moved along the riverbank taking shots of this place she might never see again. Later, changed into a bikini with sun-screen used lavishly, she strolled along the coarse, pebbly-grained sand bordering the water. A belt of trees straddling the bend of the river halted her. She moved round them to step on to the wide, flat causeway of the dam.

Dangling her feet in the coolness beneath, she allowed herself to slip lower, and lay back floating. The noise from the picnic came to her as from a distance, muffled by the screen of trees. She could have been by herself in a vast empty land.

But a figure who had been strolling among his guests had seen that sauntering form, and a frown came between fair brows. A dismissing wave was sent towards Shad, who had already begun to follow Victoria, and Scott walked after her himself.

He moved along the wide walk, then bent down to the floating girl, holding out a hand. He said, 'It's dangerous to swim here. There's an underground current running strongly beneath the dam. You'd better come out.'

Dark grey eyes looked up into a gaze of dense blue, and as brown sinewy fingers caught hold of her wrist Victoria found herself swung upwards and she was standing on the very edge of the cement. . .then her wet body met his sun-warmed one. He spoke, but the words he was saying held no meaning for her, and eyes she had up till now thought closed and guarded showed only dazzling pinpoints of concentrated brilliance. Automatically his hand went out to draw her to safety so that his fingers rested, light as thistledown, on her bare ribcage. She came to him, their gazes locked.

Her body wasn't just close to his. She felt it moulded length against length, merging, coalescing. And on the shining white pavement beneath them there was only one silhouette now. . .one single ebony outline. They stood together, bodies fused beneath a wide burning sun.

His hand remained lightly on the cool naked skin, but it was skin from which all coolness was departing as a searching wind of desire swirled about them. Seeing his head descend, her eyes closed, waiting for his kiss—a kiss that seemed a mere butterfly's touch as lips moved gently across the ones waiting to receive them.

Victoria moved, her body finding its natural harbour within his. She wasn't thinking. . .she wasn't even aware of any world around her. There was only one reality, one thought, one need—to be held close in this man's arms.

As if he had felt her movement, a ripple, a shudder passed through the form fused to hers. The light gentle kiss was suddenly no longer light, and she gasped as it scorched its caressing way to the corner of her mouth, and then down. . .down over the flung-back exposed throat.

Her hands flew up of their own accord to clasp about his neck. Drawn more completely to him, responding to the passion, the demand of those searing, branding caresses, Victoria knew that this experience, this man, was the other half of her existence.

She didn't hear a shout echoing towards them from the picnic area behind the belt of trees. The man might have done so. . .or it might have been Shad's soft voice calling.

She found herself stood away. She shook her head in

negation, opening her eyes to look up at him. They met, two glances from eyes of so different a colour, the girl's passion-hazed, the man's starkly intense for the same reason—but holding, too, another expression.

He said, 'No, Victoria. . . No!' And those light fingers on her brought her the few needed steps to safety. Then he had turned on his heel, leaving her to stand there, abandoned.

She knew he had gone; she was aware of being alone, and she turned a shaking body to walk the few steps to the other side of the dam, the wet marks her footsteps left drying almost immediately on the hard white cement.

With a hand up to shade her eyes, Victoria looked down. She saw the stream of water which Scott had mentioned when pulling her out—in another lifetime, an aeon ago—and saw also that it slithered confidently on its way towards the cloud of dark green on the far horizon. Towards the swamps of Namangilla which Geoffrey had mentioned as being so dangerous.

She drew a deep ragged breath and straightened her back. She knew what shock could do—and it was shock that was enclosing her now. She would like nothing better than to slip over this wall and be carried along that running stream to oblivion.

To offer herself! As willingly as she had done, and to be rejected! As she had been. . .in three words. Three bleak words.

Again she drew that deep necessary breath and said softly, bitterly, 'OK, Scott! Believe it! This time I'll see that I do keep out of your vicinity. What I feel about you is my bad luck, because I've never felt that way about any man before—have never wanted to be kissed and made love to like that before. But I will learn to get over it—just wait and see!'

Of course she would learn to get over it. These things had happened all through history, so if God, or fate, or karma, or whatever, had seen fit to make her fall in love with Scott Courtney, that was too bad! She would find other things to build her life on.

So, head held high, her normally smiling eyes bleak and cold, she made herself stroll carelessly back to join a crowd of people she had just met. She collected towel and clothes, and sauntered to the dressing-shed further along. She wasn't going to be swimming in any more water today.

As the day progressed, ironically she discovered that she could laugh and talk, eat a delicious lunch—or at least give an appearance of doing so. After all, this was a picnic beside flowing water on a beautiful blue and golden day.

But all she was hoping was for it to end, and finally, at long last, it was doing so. She was leaning against a big ironbark when Bobby came running. Taking hold of her hand, he looked engagingly up at her, a large smear of chocolate icing on the side of his mouth, blond hair falling over his eyes.

Absently, Victoria drew a tissue from her shorts pocket, and, holding his face steady, leaned over to wipe away the frosting.

A sensation of being watched made her glance around quickly, and the hand which was brushing the hair from the child's face fell away abruptly. A few yards from her stood two men, the fair one's eyes hooded, his expression unreadable.

She gazed back at him, hoping cool uninterest was all that was showing in her glance. The man turned away sharply, and it was the dark one who moved forward. He smiled at Victoria, his hand reaching out, and Bobby, with the naturalness of belonging, put his own small one into it.

'He's been enjoying chocolate cake,' she found herself saying a little breathlessly.

A smile lightened Shad's dark face and he said, 'Haven't we all? But I'll take him now. We're riding, and it looks as if we might be in for some bad weather.'

He half waved a hand, then moved to fall in with his silent companion. That electricity *was* there, thought Victoria defiantly, and it rode the air-waves towards her as Scott turned, walking away with that lithe jungle tread of his.

In the Jaguar on their way home, she decided that Shad had been right about the weather, when a zigzag of lightning splitting the massed clouds brought the welcoming sign of rain closer. Jagged, unbelievably brilliant, it outlined the vivid crimson and scarlet along the horizon.

Victoria helped with packing away the picnic paraphernalia, then said, 'I'm off to bed, Mrs Leith. OK?'

'Yes, of course, Victoria, but wouldn't you like a cup of tea first?'

Accepting the girl's shake of the head, she turned to Peter, who had just arrived from refuelling and checking the car after putting it away. Up here it was always refuelled immediately after use. It could be needed at a second's notice. She asked him, 'What about you, Peter?'

'Good lord, no! I'm full of food and liquid. I'm off home now. Starting at sun-up I have to get out to the northern sector.'

Victoria went to bed.

CHAPTER SIX

It RAINED for most of the next week, rain which had been sorely needed. Jennifer was out riding the paddocks with Peter and Jack, checking stock and watching for bogged animals. After his morning's work with Victoria, Geoffrey also went off to do his stint of riding the runs.

Rain *was* gold up here, but it also left behind a legacy of work. Then after a weekend of fine weather, on the Monday they had a visitor. And something came up that Victoria didn't know how to handle. The owner of the Downs had arrived.

'If the country weren't so waterlogged, Geoff, I'd send you over to Namangilla with these letters Mr Hamilton gave me for Scott,' said Mrs Leith. 'But as it is, he'll have to wait.'

'Oh, Mum, of course I could go. I've been working hard with Victoria, and working too out on the runs. Of course I could go. And I could borrow some books from Scott's library. You know he has such a lot. . .ones I like too, as well as the other sort.'

Geoffrey looked mutinous, and his mother glanced quickly at him. Victoria saw that worried gaze the older woman sometimes got where her son was concerned, so she broke in easily and, smiling, said, 'He really has been working. He'll pass that entrance exam, I promise you.'

She was unprepared for the look of gratitude sent her way, and unprepared also for the following words. . .utterly unprepared. 'Why don't you go too,

Victoria? You need to get out just as much, after being cooped up all week.'

She might need to get out, thought Victoria, but certainly not to go to the station next door. Oh, dear, no. 'Oh, I don't think so,' she was beginning easily, while her thoughts jumped round, wondering how to get herself out of this projected trip. Because of course she couldn't go. So she continued as lightly as she could manage, 'I really don't think I want to. To land there among all those men is just not my scene.'

'Scott won't be at home. . .or Shad, if that's what you mean. Probably only Old Bill and Bobby.' Geoffrey, being Geoffrey, was not going to allow a stupid idea to interfere with his outing. 'They'll be out in the paddocks working. They'll need to be searching for stock more than we have to, because there's so much more low-lying water on Namangilla.'

Victoria only shook her head. She wasn't going over to that place. However, Uncle Pete took a hand. 'I'll go and saddle you a horse, my girl; it'll do you good to have a ride,' he told her.

It would look strange to protest any more, she decided, so she could only hope that Geoffrey was right, and that the owner of Namangilla wouldn't be at home.

Home-made cakes stowed carefully beside the letters in their saddlebags, they set out. Today the ground over which they cantered was soft, sucking at their mounts' hooves. But the sun was gilding the new tips of the gums and ironbarks. The whole universe looked washed clean. Bird calls and an occasional movement of cattle were the only sounds about them. An age-old land, it slumbered untouched across the centuries that had passed it by.

The bush began to give way to more open country and eventually they reached the one place she shouldn't be going to. The Namangilla homestead sat in its cluster of trees, its frangipani, its climbing bougainvillaea and lemon-scented dwarf shrubs, with its orchard a background of vivid green and golden yellow. As for the house itself. . .

Mrs Leith had told Victoria it was a lovely homestead, and this place certainly was an old colonial mansion. Then she saw the signs of neglect; the years that standing empty showed. Victoria felt only sadness as she gazed at it. 'Geoffrey——' she began, then paused.

'What, Victoria?' he asked when she stopped.

The house seemed empty, and relief began to flood through her. Thankfully she decided that there was no one here, and that they could return home at once.

But a voice called suddenly—an old voice, anxious and strained. Geoffrey was off his horse in a flash, bridle thrown over and down.

Victoria followed more slowly. She hesitated even more as she passed inside and her gaze took in the interior. In a lounge opening off the hallway, Bobby was lying flat upon a sofa, a white rag tied tightly about his upper thigh. Old Bill was kneeling beside him holding a blood-stained bandage wrapped further down. He was speaking to Geoffrey.

'He did it with a cane knife hacking vines on the veranda. He shouldn't have been using it. I don't know what to do. . .it's so deep. . .' His old voice quivered with strain. Those dragging, unhappy words caused Victoria to move towards the couch. She had completed a first-aid course because her father had made her. She knew what should be done—but this was Scott Courtney's bailiwick, and this was also his cousin.

However, she gently lifted the bandage from under the

old man's hand, her eyes closing tightly for a swift moment at what she saw.

'Jimmy has galloped for Scott,' Old Bill was saying shakily. 'They're working near the swamp area. . . Oh, I wish he'd come!'

'Go home quickly, Geoff,' Victoria said to the boy beside her as the tired old voice stopped. 'But go carefully, because of the boggy ground. I expect they'll need to bring one of the cars back.' She knew from another conversation that Scott only owned an old farm utility. Peter had said during it, laughing, that as far as Namangilla was concerned fencing and planting grass came first, not new motor vehicles. So now she said, 'Bobby needs a doctor. Can the Flying Doctor land here after all this rain—or would it be better to go to the mission? There's a doctor there.'

Geoffrey shook his head. 'We can't get to the mission,' he told her. 'There's a washaway on the road. It would probably be better to start for the Einasleigh, but Mum would know. The Flying Doctor can land there in any weather.' His face white under the tan, he made for the door at a quick run. 'I'll go and tell Mum,' the words floated back and were succeeded by the thud of hooves receding swiftly into the distance.

'Let me,' said Victoria, and lifted the bandage again, then added, 'Have you a wide bandage?'

The old man nodded towards a box sitting on a small table beside the sofa. A family first-aid container with all the ordinary necessities—no drugs or glass phials, she noticed.

'Oh, good,' she said, turning to smile at the anxious old man. 'I want some gauze—and a square of that linen you've been using.' She took hold of both, and saw that

there was an elastic bandage rolled up in one corner of
the box. She said, her face tightening as she talked,

'Look, I want you to help me press this pad down on
the wound as tightly as we can manage. There!' Her hand
pushed the small cushion firmly against the injury and
the old fingers held it fixed on the far side. Victoria rolled
the elasticised bandage around once and pulled it as tight
as she could manage. Then carefully she continued,
making each twist as tight as she could.

Then she slowly undid the tourniquet. . .and saw dull
red staining the underside of the dressing, but stopping
before it reached the top. Her held-in breath exhaled.
Throwing the tourniquet aside, she collapsed into the
nearest chair. She remarked, hoping the words were true.
'There, I think that might hold it for a while.'

'But you'll need to tie it further up, on and off, to stop
the bleeding. . .'

'No, that's not how it's done these days. However,
we'll let Scott decide what he wants done when he gets
here,' she answered, then turned back to the little boy
with eyes now open in a face that was grey, with a small
hand tightly clasped in a gnarled, blue-veined old one.

'Would you get some tea, please, warm with plenty of
sugar?' she asked, thinking the old man would be better
off occupied, and also that what she had asked for was
what Bobby needed.

He looked at her, his expression blank, unheeding,
then back towards the other face watching from the sofa.
He stumbled to his feet.

'Yes, I'll get some—but oh, if Scott would only come,
everything would be all right.' Need for a presence he
had reason to believe could fix anything sounded in the
faltering words.

Victoria wished Scott would come too. He wasn't Scott

Courtney any more, who, in one brief minute of eternity, had set her life on a different path. He was someone who could take to himself the responsibility for this young boy. Her glance followed Old Bill as he left, then went back to check the tell-tale bandage. How long would Geoffrey be? Over an hour to get home, riding as fast as he dared; not as long to return by car.

Her glance fell on a table already set for a night-time dinner, and she gazed almost with incredulity at exquisitely embossed silver that glittered and gleamed back at her. . . Apparently one legacy, it seemed, that had not been stripped from Namangilla. It made her look further, and she saw furniture that matched it—heavy, solid, bequeathed down the ages; its patina soft, lustrous, gleaming as the silver did in the large high-ceilinged room.

The paint on the walls showed mildew and flaking strips, but the room's contents were a collector's dream. Could this be the reason for Scott's rejection of her? she wondered. Most likely his plans included a daughter from one of the other big properties up here, to add the finishing touch to Namangilla. Well, good luck to him. She would get over this unlooked-for episode in her life.

Old Bill, suddenly beside her, was holding out a cup and a long spoon. So, with a hand behind it, Victoria held the small head firmly as the man spooned the warm sweet liquid slowly between pallid lips. Halfway through, while she was wiping some spilled drops from the small grey face, there came the thunder of hooves—right up to the very veranda edge. Abruptly, the owner of Namangilla was in the room, a dark shadow behind him.

Immediately he was kneeling beside Bobby, and Shad was walking to a high shelf. He was back instantly with a white box, its red cross boldly outlined, and somehow

Victoria found herself across the room on a chair by the dinner-set table.

There came the sickening smell of ether drifting over to where she sat, strong, pungent, causing nausea to well, and then consciousness was a whirling Catherine wheel, going faster and faster.

She threw out an arm to ward it off and the next she knew her head was almost on the floor, with a vicelike hand holding it there. For a long minute that clasp held, then was relaxed, two hands on her shoulders bringing her upright.

'All right now?' a voice called calmly.

Angry with herself for allowing this to happen, she said sharply. 'Yes, of course I'm all right. Despite my name, I'm really not a Victorian miss to be overcome by the sight of a little blood.'

'I'm sure you're not, but there was more than a little blood,' that same voice answered just as calmly.

'Yes!' A shudder went through her body and she glanced quickly towards the couch. There had indeed been more than a little blood. Bobby was now wrapped in a blanket and he seemed unconscious—whether from being made so, or naturally, she didn't know.

'Your father's teaching, I expect—your knowing what to do?' Again that easy, impersonal voice spoke from above her head, then it paused, as Shad leaned over to hand her a cup from which a spiral of vapour was rising. She glanced at both faces above her, and smelling the spirits made no attempt to take the drink.

It was the dark face that spoke. 'You need it. Drink it up,' it said.

So she slowly sipped the fortified tea, while the fair man stood there, patiently waiting for an answer to his question. She said, with her face in the cup, 'I suppose so. He made both my sister and me attend first-aid classes.'

As if satisfied, Scott asked, 'Do you think you could hold Bobby's leg as it should be held while I drive to the Einasleigh?'

'Look, if it was only a case of holding his leg, of course I could. But you'd be better off with Mrs Leith. She'd know more than I——'

'I think you've shown that you know enough,' came the reply.

Victoria stared. This was Scott Courtney, and she knew what his thoughts of her were. She still answered, 'I might have applied some first aid, but——'

Again she was not allowed to finish. 'Shad's been on the radio and has been told the Flying Doctor can't land either here or at the Leiths', but that he's already on his way to attend to another patient at the Einasleigh, where he can land in all weathers. So we'll try for there!'

Victoria didn't want to go anywhere with him, remembering that scene on the dam wall where she had been so flatly rejected. However, that self-assured figure was saying politely, as pleasantly as he had been speaking all the time, 'If Peter's returned, you won't be needed, but if it's only Mrs Leith. . .' The words stopped, then continued, 'I'll have to drive, and Shad has to get back to where we were working.'

She found suddenly that her head was nodding without her telling it to, and while it was in the yes position there came the sound of an engine, loud in the evening dusk.

In a split second all was motion. Shad had picked up the small swathed body, Scott a long slim container from the big white one. So, rising to her feet, Victoria followed the man carrying the blanketed bundle.

It was Mrs Leith driving, in the Jaguar, not Peter with

the four-wheeled Land Rover. 'Look, Scott,' she was saying breathlessly, 'I hope you can get there in this. Peter has the Land Rover away and it would take too long to find him, even if this car could get there. The road to the Einasleigh might not be good, but it *is* a road, so OK?'

'As you say, it is a road, and we'll manage. Thanks, Mrs Leith.' Scott smiled at the older woman, who only nodded anxiously back, then he opened the back door and indicated for Victoria to enter.

Wanting to or not—and she didn't—she automatically did as that gesture bade her. She found herself on the seat with Bobby being manoeuvred in to rest on her lap.

Scott was in behind the wheel in one swift lithe movement. He spoke a few last words to Shad, who only nodded, and they were on their way.

Often in years to come Victoria would recall that nightmare ride—for it was a nightmare. The road was a horror, the sun had gone, twilight finding its way into night all too swiftly.

She sat and worried about Bobby's leg as the car fled across washaways, over potholes, sailing through small gullies still running with the drain-off of a week's soaking rain.

A slight movement from her lap made her lean over and say, 'Are you all right, love?' There came no reply.

Over a shoulder, his attention concentrated on the tunnel of light before him, Scott asked, 'Did he want something?'

'I don't know. I thought he moved, but he doesn't answer. Would it be the pain, do you think?'

'I'll stop in a few minutes. We'll soon be in better country.' And in the few minutes he had mentioned, the car did stop. As he stepped out, Victoria saw their driver silhouetted. The moon had risen.

He was bending over the supine form, saying, 'How goes it, mate? We'll be in the Einasleigh in half an hour. You'll be right then.'

There came no answer, but Victoria thought she felt a stirring of the small figure.

Moonlight glinted silver-gilt on a bare head as it came upright and departed. Then, on their way again, Victoria began to think that half-hour which Scott had mentioned would never pass. Her legs had gone numb and she was terrified to move or stretch in case she restarted the bleeding.

Then, almost not believing it, out of a void of darkness, she saw lights swimming towards them. Not glaring city illuminations, certainly, but civilisation of a kind, none the less.

Before a building with light streaming out, they came to a stop, and two men came quickly down some steps. Bobby was caught up between them and carried away, Scott following.

Endeavouring to straighten her legs, Victoria caught back a cry. Biting her lips, she tried to massage the cramp away. The ball of ridged tissue contracted, hard, agonising. She groped her way out of the seat, hanging on to the wide-swinging door. . .and suddenly tensed. An arm had gone round her doubled-up body, an arm which, even at this time, sent a tremor of tension through her.

'I'm OK,' Victoria spoke brusquely. 'It's only a cramp, but I——'

'Of course you're OK!' The reply came matter-of-factly. 'But cramp is cramp, and no respecter of persons. Here, let me.'

Scott knelt in the roadway and massaged the leg she was still unable to stand on. The rigid knots disappeared under iron-hard fingers, kneaded away with expert thoroughness and no gentleness at all.

'Thank you!' The two words came gasping as he stood upright.

'Be my guest,' was all the reply she received. 'We were lucky that the doctor was already here. All we have to do now is wait,' Scott told her as they passed inside. He sat beside her while they waited, but he remained silent, unmoving, leaning against the wall at his back.

He looked tired, Victoria thought. Of course he would look tired. He'd probably been out working in the paddocks all day, and he'd had that dreadful drive. . .

She glanced at the shadows darkening his eyes, and unexpectedly he seemed older than the young, arrogantly confident man she had always thought him. Suddenly she wondered how old he actually was. He had been away all those long years, and back here for three, so he must be. . . Abruptly, on this night and evening when there had been not even the semblance of a smile, she grinned. It was a grin entirely at herself. She could imagine Scott's reaction if she did what she would like to do—reached out a hand to smooth that fair hair from his forehead, saying, 'Rest for a while until they come to bring us word.' Lord! That would take some imagining!

'What's the matter?' She jumped, literally. Those blue eyes had swung round, looking directly at her as he asked his question.

'What do you mean?' countered Victoria. 'Nothing's the matter.'

'Something seemed to be a moment ago.' He glanced down at her outstretched legs and added, 'Is that cramp worrying you? It comes back sometimes if the muscles have been contracted too long.'

'No. . .no, it's gone. I was only thinking about Bobby.' That lie would do as well as any other.

'He should be all right. He's a healthy little boy, and you did all the right things. Thank you, Victoria.'

She didn't answer. What could she reply to those words? She was rescued from wondering as a woman entered. Smiling, she told them, 'I've brought you some tea,' and set down the tray she was carrying.

They drank the tea, and Scott even took up a sandwich, but he wasn't eating it, Victoria noticed. Then, setting down his cup, he rose to prowl restlessly up and down the room. Presently he went away. He said to her over a shoulder, 'I'll just see. . .' The sentence was left unfinished.

Returning in quite a short time, he was telling her, the tension seemingly all gone, 'The doctor informs me Bobby should be playing with cane-knives again in a week or so, Victoria. I'm off to see him now. I'll only be a minute.'

She replied quickly, relief showing, 'He really is going to be all right, then?'

'Right as rain,' answered Scott as he made for the doorway, then paused to add, 'Of course, doctors being a cautious race, he qualified that statement with the usual warnings. But that's doctors for you!'

He was back in quite a short time. 'He looks fine, and they're keeping him here for the night. So we can stop worrying and make tracks for home. Come along.'

There was no nightmare rush on the return journey. Scott sent them slowly and carefully along. Leaning back in her own corner, Victoria watched a countryside outlined in silver slide past. From under downcast lashes she turned to look at her driver, wondering what that silent figure was thinking.

He had said to her once, 'No, Victoria,' and walked away. Tonight he was a different man entirely. Oh, well, there was tomorrow, and it always came.

Almost home, Scott switched off the engine some distance away, allowing the Jaguar to coast gently down the incline to the garage.

CHAPTER SEVEN

OPENING her own door, Victoria stepped from the car unaided. She said when Scott came round to stand beside her, 'There's no need for you to come up to the house with me. It's just the few yards, and you'll want to get home.'

With fingers reaching out to lightly clasp an elbow, barely touching it, he said, 'Yes, there is. Snakes go searching for their food in the silence and stillness of the night, and I wouldn't want you to stand on one.'

She wouldn't want to stand on one either; she wasn't afraid of them, but she didn't like them, so, walking gingerly beside him, she went up to the house.

He did not ask which was her room; he did not guide her to the front of the house. Those light fingers brought her to stand on the veranda before her own doorway. Of course! He had known this place all his life. He would know the layout of the house, and where the family slept.

And then she wasn't thinking of mundane affairs at all. Scott had taken her by her elbows. He didn't bring her to him, and they stood in the bright moonlight facing one another, the space of yards between them.

He said, 'Thank you, Victoria' and bending, put his mouth on hers. The kiss he bestowed was gentle, a small gesture to say his thanks. Nothing more—she knew that! But suddenly she didn't care. She swayed forward. However, those iron-hard horseman's hands kept her away, and he said softly, 'I've said no to you once before, Victoria, and,' here a small derisive laugh sounded before he continued, 'then, as now, don't think I didn't want to make love to you. I did then. I do now! But my life is mapped out, my decisions made. There can be no future for us together. You must understand that completely.'

She knew he wasn't married, and that was the only consideration that would have halted the way she went to him; to this man who was the other half of her life. The soft curves of her body fused into the hardness of flesh and bone, into the rigidity of corded muscles. For the fraction of a second she felt the hesitation, the indecision that struck through his whole form. Then his hand was spreadeagled low on her back, bringing her entirely to him. His head came down, and this time he was kissing her with no reservation at all.

This time also there was no stopping those jumping pulses of desire that were uncoiling deep within her. She pressed closer, allowing mind and body to float as the slow, heartbreaking caresses dissolved the brilliant night about her into a whirling cataclysm of need. . . passion. . .

She found herself swung up, and she was being carried unerringly through the door into her room. Depositing her on the bed, Scott sat too, an arm inflexibly straight on either side, keeping her prisoner. He wasn't kissing her now, but she could both hear and feel so close to her the ragged rhythm of his breathing.

He bent over her, and a voice that was not Scott's said, 'I'm no teenage youth, Victoria. Do you realise what you're setting in motion? Because when I start to make love to you in this fashion, it will go the whole way. Do you understand what I'm saying?'

She could only nod, then she said, 'I don't care, Scott!'

'OK. . .' He swung her over and slid down beside her, bringing her length to meet his. She lay, knowing that this was Scott, who had given her his conditions, and that tomorrow she would have to think about them. . .come to terms with them. But for tonight they were dismissed.

And then any thinking had gone with the wind. Scott had leaned across her and his lips were moving gently back and forth upon her own. In no hurry, they paused at the corner of her mouth and then went on to travel along a throat, exposed, thrown back, to pause for a moment on a starkly jumping pulse.

She gasped, and her breathless voice said, 'Scott. . .'

He didn't answer. He didn't stop those plundering lips either, as they moved on to leave trailing rivers of fire in their wake. Victoria's body arched and the thin gold chain around her neck ran glittering and gleaming in a striking shaft of moonlight.

She had never been made love to like this before; she was only following where Scott was leading, and her whole body jumped as long tanned fingers began to follow along the path his lips had already broken. She didn't experience for that first moment the suddenness of his withdrawal from her until a hand reached out to clasp her shoulder.

Then, unexpectedly, for a long second there came no movement to disturb the silence in the moonlight-flooded room. Scott came up on an elbow. 'Victoria?' he said, and that familiar voice carried no easy pleasantness now. Strain and harshness coloured it.

'Victoria,' he repeated, and her name spoken in that so different voice sounded strange too. 'I'm sorry, I thought. . .but I realise now that I was wrong.'

Startled at those words, Victoria remained silent.

He said again, 'I *was* wrong, wasn't I?'

Unerringly, she knew what he meant, but what was

she to answer? Should she lie? And then she knew that
with Scott if he found out—and he would—he would
walk away completely from her.

'Victoria!' His one word, and that tone, asked for the
third time for an answer.

'Does it matter what kind of experience I've had? I
love you, Scott!'

'Yes, it does matter.'

Scott was the only man she would ever love, so she
said, 'I'm not a teenager either. I know what I'm doing.'

'Well, you're not doing it with me.' He had turned
away from her, lying flat on his back, arms stretched
loosely by his sides.

At least, a little voice whispered to her, he hadn't
turned and walked away, as he had done that other time.
She remained silent, endeavouring to think of something,
anything, that would show him. . .

But she didn't need to speak. It was her companion
who was doing so, and she lay immobile, trying to take
in the meaning of what he was saying. . .the incredible
words. 'More than anything,' that soft silken voice was
saying, 'I want to make love to you. . . More than
anything I want to hold you completely in my arms. . .'

Here, one hand unexpectedly slid beneath her, bringing her to lie closely within his clasp, to face him as he
continued, 'But I know if this affair is allowed to get
serious what it would entail. Although you may say at
this time—at this moment—that it doesn't matter, that
you don't care. . . I've had experience of the havoc
caused by transplanting one way of life to an entirely
different one. . .'

These words came to her from only inches away, and
she gazed into those eyes she knew so well, but which
were now just dark hollows against the shaft of moonlight

behind him, and she knew absolutely that with this man, only what he intended to happen would happen. . .only what his will decided would prevail.

Then abruptly, in an entirely different tone, other words came to her. 'But of course,' he was saying, and in those shadowed cornflower-blue eyes, dancing pinpoints of brilliance were suddenly showing, moonlight caught within them as he turned his gaze. 'But of course,' he was repeating, 'there are always other spheres of activity that we might explore together.'

Victoria moved away from that body so close, from that suggestive voice. He could mean what anyone chose to think he meant—but with Scott using that tone you never knew. So she said, 'I might once have been in love with you, Scott Courtney, but I now find that circumstances can change one's feelings. I have no intention at all of exploring anything with you. I'd like you to go.'

Scott didn't move to depart. He reached out a hand to touch her, and, jerking away, she slid off the bed. Furious at this indignity, trying to rise, she was aware of a body dropping down beside her.

She didn't laugh; she wasn't in the mood for laughing, but she felt the ripple that shook the heavy form against her and knew that it was silent, shaking laughter that was issuing from him. Fists clenched in anger on identifying it were taken hold of and clasped tightly while he told her, 'I'm not laughing at you, Victoria. I'm laughing at myself,' and there was the ghost of amusement still echoing before he added more seriously,

'In any of my. . .liaisons, shall we say, I've always been able to stand aside knowing exactly what I'm doing; but with you. . . Oh, with you! Now, if I free your hands will you try not to kill me, because we'll have to talk seriously? But tonight, with all the trauma and tension we've been through, is certainly not the time.' He released her hands.

'No,' answered Victoria carefully, 'I won't try to kill you, and no, I also don't want to have a talk with you. All I want is for you to go. You were right the other day on that high cement wall—I accept it now.'

Tiredly, her whole body collapsed; and in the same instant Scott's arm went around her, cradling her to him.

They lay there, figures entwined. Then, up on one knee, Scott moved to swing her into his arms, and, turning to the bed, deposited her on the pillows.

He sat beside her with arms stretched on either side. He remained silent for a moment, then said, 'Victoria!'

With no answer forthcoming, he said again, 'Victoria, I'd arranged my life. I've known for so many years the way it was going to go. But you've been thrown into that life, causing ripples to spread in all directions.' Scott's voice stopped for a moment and Victoria stirred restlessly, but the iron-hard arms keeping her a prisoner remained firm as he continued speaking.

'However, I found that you seemed to like being up here, that you appeared happy as you went about preparing that alfresco lunch you shared with me. But telling me off about who you'd rather eat with was the turning-point. That doesn't often happen, my being who I am, and Namangilla what it is.'

What Namangilla was didn't worry her. What he was was an entirely different matter. 'No, I don't suppose it does,' she answered, and without warning all indignation and anger had vanished. All she wanted was this night to be over, this man gone.

He was saying quietly, 'We need a breathing-space, Victoria, you as much as me,' and abruptly his imprisoning arms were removed. He straightened up.

However, the girl beneath him was thinking tiredly
that no, they didn't need any breathing-space. She had
decided that this short, fiercely burning love would have
to be forgotten. She said again, tiredly, 'Please go, Scott.
I find now that all I want to do is prepare Geoffrey for
his exam and then leave this place. Please go,' she asked
for a second time.

Scott had lifted one of his arms to trail the back of his
fingers gently down her cheek. Victoria closed her eyes.
She wasn't going to cry. Determinedly she pushed back
the tears which that gentle gesture had caused to start.

Then one of her hands was taken, the fingers prised
open, and into the outspread palm the man dropped a
kiss. He shut it carefully, then without another word he
was gone—and, as was his custom, leaving no sound at
all of his going.

All the passionate desire, the conflict of a few moments
ago had drained away, and tiredly Victoria swung her
legs off the bed to go to stand in the doorway. Without
volition one hand still remained firmly closed as if
remembering the feel of lips which had touched it.

Her gaze travelled towards the garage, thinking he
would most likely take the Jaguar as it was quieter. But
no sound came to her waiting ears.

Then further down, in the distance, two shadows,
ebony-dark in the brilliance of the night, detached themselves from the railed-in stockyards. Even as she looked,
the two images became one. No sound came to her as
both horse and rider merged into the night, but unexpectedly there came a gleam of brightness, as if moonlight
had caught and held for that one brief moment a carelessly turned golden head.

She turned away unhappily, and undressed, allowing

the clothes to lie where they fell, then with a short cotton nightdress pulled over her head climbed wearily into bed.

What was she to do? She couldn't leave. As she had told Scott, Geoffrey needed her. But what could she do? It wasn't fair, she decided. She need never have come up here.

Well, she would see what tomorrow brought. Tomorrow she might find she didn't care. For tonight. . . She turned restlessly, and found her face pressed against a pillow where a man's head had rested—and Scott was suddenly there beside her once again.

Hot, scorching tears found their way down her cheeks, and she wiped them angrily away with the back of her fists. How had it been allowed to happen. . .the disintegration of what could have been a wonderful love-story?

The tears fell faster until, exhausted, she turned her face into the pillow, and lay with a shaft of moonlight outlining the arm curled round it, the tear-stained face buried deep.

Next morning Shad rode over with the Leith horse and a thank-you from Scott. In the weeks that followed, the Einasleigh trip and its aftermath was pushed resolutely from the mind of one of the participants. Of the other there was no sign at all.

As it was now monsoon weather, it caused no surprise when the rain returned. Then one night, in a brightly lit kitchen, all heads were raised from the dinner table as there came the sound of a horse travelling swiftly through a rain-sodden night.

The figure that presently stood in the kitchen doorway might have been expected by some, but was totally unexpected by Victoria.

'Hello, Scott. Have you eaten?' asked Mrs Leith, then added, 'How's Bobby?'

'Yes, thanks to the first, and it's taking threats to keep Bobby from behaving the way any seven-year-old with two solid legs behaves. I'm on my way to one of my out-boundaries, but I turned aside to let you know the river's coming down. In fact I thought I heard it as I cut across the bend. You might be able to see it; the clouds are breaking and there's a faint moonlight.'

'I'm coming!' Swallowing whatever his mouth was holding, Geoffrey was out of his chair, and below corn-yellow wind-tossed hair, blue eyes turned towards Victoria.

'Would you like to go, Victoria?' asked Mrs Leith. 'I don't expect you've ever seen a river come down?'

Not knowing what was meant by a river coming down, Victoria merely shook her head.

'Off you go then—it's something you shouldn't miss. Now you be careful, Geoffrey,' Mrs Leith added sharply to her son and heir as he hurled himself headlong from the room.

In the doorway, half turned to the outside, Scott waited. Unsure of him, Victoria remained seated.

'Get a raincoat from the rack, Victoria,' said her employer. So, obeying because she wanted to, Victoria slid her arms into the first one she could reach.

They sloshed along the beaten path on the top of the riverbank, Geoffrey diving ahead of them. Hands thrust deep into the pockets of the old coat, Victoria wondered why. . .but why didn't matter just now, she decided, and raising her face to the sky she breathed deeply, amazed at the things that happiness could be made of. Just to be here, just to be walking alongside Scott, even. . .

Although, remembering what had passed between them on their last time together. . .

Clouds were scudding from horizon to horizon, wind-tossed, showing only an occasional glimpse of clear heavens. Fitful, storm-tossed still, they showed nature in the wild—primitive, turbulent, civilisation a puny creation far away. No lights showed. There was not a glimpse even of the house they had just left.

Suddenly, from out of the night, Victoria heard a sound; eerie, weird. Scott drew her off the path towards the cliff top, lower here than their own escarpment by the house. He spoke sharply to Geoffrey, who had picked up a broken branch to cast out into the darkness beneath them.

'Come back a bit! If you overbalance, your mother would hound me out of Queensland!'

Louder by the second, the strange, almost frightening sound was coming nearer. Involuntarily Victoria moved closer to the solid, safe familiar form beside her. An arm went round plastic-enclosed shoulders; an utterly impersonal arm. Even through that queer noise echoing all about them, she recognised that fact.

'Here it comes,' said Scott, and as if to bestow its blessing a thin crescent of new moon sailed free from its clothing of clouds to show a wall of water rushing down the river bed. Victoria had thought—if she had thought at all on the subject—that when rivers came down, the water in them rose higher. She had never imagined anything like this, or the primitive sound that unleashed water racing down a constricted channel could make.

Fascinated, she saw the torrent rushing towards her like an extra-high ocean wave. Unlike an ocean wave, however, this wall of frightening energy didn't crash and then recede, and she stood gazing at its swirling might as it swept past. Scott's arm was an iron-hard band holding her safe.

'It's quite something, isn't it?' said her companion pleasantly, and the clasp went away.

Yes, she thought, it *was* quite something!

'She'll be running a banker tomorrow, won't she, Scott?' Geoff was saying excitedly. 'And so will your little river. . . And all your billabongs will be flooded.'

'Yes, I expect they will,' came the answer, with an added, 'There you are, Victoria—you've seen your first river come down! But the clouds are coming back. We'll be drenched if we don't watch out.'

On the back veranda, helping her off with the too large raincoat, Scott's arms encircled her for a heartbeat of time.

Victoria moved away. She didn't know how to take this man. Then from a short distance beyond her, he was telling her quietly, 'I've got to go up to the big smoke for a few days. Against all my resolutions I'm coming to see you when I get back. Will that be all right with you?' A new tone had come to colour the words of this last sentence.

Unable to help herself, she heard the two-worded answer she gave to him. 'Very well.'

She found herself drawn back, the warm length of his body holding her to him. Her eyes fell shut. Whatever Scott's attitude to her; whatever his decisions on future commitments, she was where she was meant to be, because this man was the reason for her existence.

She felt rather than heard the deep breath he took. Then she was being propelled towards the brightly lit kitchen. Thankfully she took the cup Mrs Leith was handing to her, cuddling its warmth to her. She heard Scott say, 'I've got a lift in the Hamilton plane on

Monday when the twins go back to the university. You're going too, Peter, aren't you?'

'Yes, and Joanna's coming.'

'No, she isn't. She's already left. An offer of a vacation job came up, I believe.'

That was all he said, but beginning to know him now, and all the different tones his voice could carry, Victoria wondered what that unknown nuance she heard in it meant. She wondered, too, why he was going to the city.

Then as if he had tuned in on her thoughts, Scott said quietly, 'I'm going to Townsville on business that should have been attended to before this; but I expect that for now I'd better set about the business of running my station. I'm off to check on the north boundary. So long!'

He left, and as she walked to the sink to run her cup under the tap, Victoria's thoughts were of the beautiful Joanna. . .who would also be in the city. But Scott had said. . .he *had* said, hadn't he? Her hand clenching on the cup she was holding, she remembered the words he had spoken: 'More than anything I want to make love to you; more than anything I want to hold you completely. . .' He *had* said those words to her. She shook her head sharply and reached for a tea-towel.

Suddenly she thought, what did she care what he was going to the city for? This night had not been wasted; she had seen a river come down. And when he came back. . . She hardly heard Jennifer say, 'I'm going off to listen to that radio play, anyone else coming?' as she went off to the little study used for book-keeping and the radios.

However, Victoria followed, and later, on her way to bed, she tried to get events of the night clear in her mind. Why had Scott turned aside to show her the spectacle of a river in flood? Why had he held her as he had done out on the veranda? She came to a halt just inside her door, feeling again the tension, the static electricity which had fused their two bodies when she had stood, her back lying against him. Well, time marched on, whether wanted or unwanted, and Scott had said he would see her when he got back.

She went to bed.

CHAPTER EIGHT

MONDAY morning came and, standing outside beside Mrs Leith, Victoria saw the fair-headed man arrive. She returned the wave both he and Peter sent their way as the Land Rover leaped forward. Her glance followed it until it was no longer in sight, then she turned sharply, gazing down fixedly at the tumbling waters below.

Long slivers of light from the newly risen sun gilded the swirling river into molten gold as it ran high and swift upon its journey into the unknown. Waters which she had first seen crashing along down there while, on an escarpment high above, an iron-hard arm held her safe and protected. Sighing, she turned and followed the older woman into the house.

Ten days later, Scott arrived again without warning. As he came to stand in the kitchen doorway, five pairs of eyes swivelled sharply towards him.

He seemed different, was Victoria's first thought as she took in a head still damp from the shower; hair on it that not even a ride through a night already alive with the evening breeze had disturbed.

His glance roved the room; he saw her, but his look passed on. Victoria felt a shiver, a *frisson* as her nerves reacted to that look. She pulled her hands from the table and clasped them tightly together below it. There *was* something different about him. . .and whatever it was it in some way concerned her.

'Good evening, Mrs Leith,' he spoke first to his hostess, then turned to Peter. 'I expected to find you here and not at your own place. Those smoke signals, I expect, that everyone up here says I have.'

He was smiling, and the flash of white showed starkly against skin which seemed a darker brown than normal, against hair shining almost silver-gilt instead of corn-yellow gold. Apparently he'd been out in a blazing sun much more than he usually was.

'Everything fixed for that expedition of ours,' he was telling Peter. 'Say thank you nicely.'

Peter was grinning, apparently happy at whatever it was that was fixed. Scott was continuing, 'I wondered, Mrs Leith, if you'd allow Jennifer and Geoffrey, with Victoria, to come to Chillagoe for the weekend? I bought a Land Rover while I was in Townsville, and it will be on Friday's train for me to collect.'

With Mrs Leith not answering immediately, Scott was adding, 'Victoria should see the caves at Chillagoe before she leaves the district, and it would be nice for Bobby to have Geoffrey.'

Mrs Leith glanced across at him, and, sitting silent, Victoria wondered at the reason for this invitation. He might be collecting a Land Rover, but why take them all? Of course it could be a kind of thank-you for her help with Bobby that night.

Scott *had* said he would talk to her when he got back, and he had also said to her once that he always spoke only the truth. Anyway, why worry about the reason? She was going to take what was offered when it was offered, and when life presented the bill—as it always did—pay it.

Inadvertent thoughts scattered suddenly on the wind when Scott started speaking again. He said, 'I promise to take good care of them. . .not to drive carelessly—and see that they go to bed early.' He was laughing at the older woman, and Victoria thought, It's not fair! He just has to look that certain way, act that certain way, and we all say yes.

Then, in his brash manner, Geoffrey was having his say. 'Oh, do say yes, Mum! Not that I want to go through the silly old caves, I've been through them lots of times, but a new Land Rover to have a go at—wow!'

'Cast your cotton-picking thoughts off the Rover, my boy! You won't be doing any driving—I don't want it driven up a tree or into a washaway. I've found that accidents with cane-knives have a way of turning up, so I want to be prepared next time.'

Mrs Leith nodded at these words, while giving a grateful glance around her own family. Then, as she began to speak on another subject altogether, her voice collided with her daughter's who was saying determinedly, 'I think it's a beaut idea.' So, outgunned, her mother shrugged acquiescence.

'I'll be off, then.' Scott's words were directed at Peter as he turned to leave. 'Pick us up early on Saturday morning. OK?'

Peter pushed back his chair and followed him outside. Mrs Leith began to pack dishes, and Victoria reached for the scattered silver.

'The caves are quite a tourist attraction, Victoria,' her employer was saying. 'I'm pleased you're going to visit them. It would be a crime to be actually up here and not go. I suppose, also, that I'm going to have to think about Jennifer and Peter. He's been so good about things, while Jennifer's only determined to get her own way. . .' Mrs Leith's voice trailed off. Victoria could spare no sympathy for her. Everyone had their troubles. At least Jennifer knew where she stood.

So on Saturday morning they drove through a bush

just coming alive with the dawn, with a rising sun sending forth its golden wings of the morning. The Courtney homestead, when they reached it, seemed a familiar place to Victoria after the trauma and worry she had experienced within it.

Peter jumped down, smile a mile wide on his face as he said, 'OK, bestir yourself, Victoria, you're riding in the back.'

So she went round to the rear of the Rover and was helped up the high treads, where Bobby and Old Bill joined them. 'Here's a brownie, missy,' the old man said, handing her up a cloth-wrapped package.

'It's still hot, Victoria,' exclaimed Bobby, jigging up and down with excitement, 'and Old Bill's brownies are beaut! You'll see at morning teatime.'

Victoria went to smile at him, then he was abruptly wiped from her mind. The engine had burst into life, and Peter was taking off in his customary way, gravel spurting from beneath the wheels, and Scott had stepped up the high treads and swung inside.

He stood for a moment, swaying to the rock of the vehicle, arm raised to hold on to a roof strut for support while he looked down at her. She met that steady, dense blue gaze, her own glance as blank as she could make it. Then he had dropped down beside her, and for a brief moment the side of his body, the hard length of his thigh, was lying closely against her own. Then it had shifted and he was just another passenger.

She had resolved she would let Scott set the tone of this expedition. He had said, hadn't he, that he would see her when he got back? Well, he was seeing her now, even if it wasn't in private, and glancing sideways at him she saw that extra-dark profile starkly outlined against the sunlit window.

Breaking the tanned symmetry of the smooth sun-
glazed skin were tiny creases running from eye to temple,
and what she had not noticed before, because they were
so fair, were unnaturally long lashes, resting now over
half-shut, intense blue eyes. Then, as if he felt her gaze,
Scott's head moved and she saw. . . She gave a deep
indrawn breath and sharply turned her glance from that
omniscient, considering look. She gazed out of the
window beside her.

There was no awkwardness, however, in the big vehicle as it bounded its way along the rutted bush track
towards this ghost town to which they were going. There
was laughter and soft talk echoing from the front where
Jennifer and Peter were making the most of this day they
had been given. And in the back, of course, there was no
silence—Geoffrey was in it.

Victoria just sat taking her happiness from the presence
of the man beside her, deciding that, like Jennifer, she
too would make the best of this day which she also had
been given. The Rover began to slow, and while Victoria
was wondering why the others were out of the vehicle the
moment it stopped.

'Come along, Victoria. Morning teatime,' the eldest
one said, and put up a hand to help her.

'Boil the billy, Peter. That'd be beaut,' called Geoffrey.

'Not today—we haven't time. I'm afraid we'll have to
borrow from civilisation this morning, and drink tea from
a Thermos.' It was Scott answering, but Peter was
speaking too.

'OK, it's safe to sit on,' he said, indicating a fallen
tree-trunk he had been stamping around. So the two girls
sat on the log's warm surface, and, squeezing between
them, Bobby mumbled through a mouthful he was
chewing,

'Eat your brownie, Victoria, while it's warm. It's yummy.'

Victoria bit into her slice; it tasted of fruit and exotic spices—just the food to be eating on a blue and golden day by the side of a bushland road. It blended in with the tang of gum leaves, the freshness of the early morning.

Then she wasn't thinking of edible things. Scott had dropped down beside her. 'Tea tastes better out of an enamel mug, I always think,' he remarked, but his glance was not on the girl he was speaking to. Half closed, it was on the branches of a tall ironbark that swayed above them against a lapis lazuli sky.

'I've never drunk out of one before,' answered Victoria, and slowly sipped from the container they were discussing. It could have been bone china and she would not have noticed the difference. This was Scott sitting beside her, publicly selecting his position, behaving as would any young man intent on enjoying himself.

On their way again, the swiftly moving wheels sent the miles behind them, and Victoria found that she too could manage to take part in the conversation, acting normally as she would have done on any other familiar outing at home. Then Scott said, 'The old chimney should be on the skyline at any moment.'

A ghost town now, Chillagoe had once been the centre for a far northern outback, but with the coming of the depression only one hotel and a few government buildings hinted at a time gone beyond recall. Astride it all reared the huge chimney. Stark and immense, it suggested desertion, desolation.

'You girls are here; the boys next door, with Scott and me around the corner,' said Peter, as he led them upstairs after checking in at the hotel. He added, 'Now get a move on, then bring them downstairs, Jennifer—you know your way around this place.'

Victoria grinned as she glanced about their accommodation. The room had all the necessary furniture, but it was a long way from the almost obligatory motel luxury one received when travelling nowadays. She heard the boys talking in the next room, then Geoffrey's head popped round their door. 'I'm hungry,' he said. 'How about lunch, Jen?'

'When I'm ready,' answered his sister, and became busy with a lipstick.

'I'll just see if Bobby's OK,' said Victoria, and went out of their room and into the next one. Bobby was just sitting quietly, not acting at all like his normal lively self. But she only said, 'Come along, Bobby. We're going downstairs.'

Downstairs, seeing the two men coming through the dining-room doorway, Geoffrey was demanding, 'Have you got it already, Scott?'

Scott pushed him down into a seat, but it was Peter who was answering. 'Of course we have! As it was for Scott! Now if it had been for me. . . One wonders. . .'

'Use your mouth for other things—like eating,' said Scott curtly, then added, 'The last tour for the caves has already left, so are there any other suggestions?'

There were all sorts. And outside, inspecting the Rovers—the new and the old—Victoria thought ironically, listening to the car talk, that the new one looked hardly any different from the old, except for being just a little shinier. Men—and their preoccupation with motor engines!

Then a tanned hand was being held out to her, and her fingers went into Scott's, as she was swung into the passenger seat of the new Rover. He *had* changed, she decided, then watched as, with that fluid movement she remembered, he swung up behind the wheel. His hand rested against her outstretched leg as he reached to switch on. She looked down at it. A hand was only a hand; anyone's hand, she told herself bleakly. . .and knew so differently!

They cruised along what once had been a main street before turning off. Then their driver pulled the vehicle to a stop in front of a cliff of stone rising abruptly, instantly from the ground, its vast jumble of giant rocks outlined in fantastic shapes against the tropical blue of the sky.

'Are these the caves you all keep talking about, Scott?' she exclaimed.

Her companion laughed, and Victoria swung round. She had never before heard him laugh out loud. She had seen—and felt—him laugh silently, yes; she had seen him amused, yes, but she had not heard this happy, enjoying-himself sound from him before. His blue eyes met her dark grey ones.

'No, Victoria,' he answered. 'This is merely a bluff.' She looked with fascination at the vast jumble of incredible rocks, but then they were gone, as her driver swung the Rover in a sharp turn.

Geoffrey's voice came to claim their attention from the back. 'Take us up behind the old smelters, Scott. I haven't seen the chimney from close up.'

They saw the chimney from close up, and Victoria thought sadly when, later, Scott ran in behind Peter's vehicle at the hotel, that happy times always flew. They left the men to put the cars to bed and the two girls made their way upstairs.

Jennifer ran up the steps before Victoria, then, flopping down on one of the beds, lay outspread with her head resting against the wall. 'Aren't I glad you're here, Victoria?' she exclaimed, grinning.

On her bed on the other side of the room, lying back too, Victoria raised her eyebrows. Jennifer had only treated her casually as another visitor to the station— friendly, certainly, but quite uninterested. So why these words?

As she replied to that look of enquiry, Jennifer's grin turned into a laugh. 'If you had seen the caves,' she answered, 'and if you hadn't helped Scott with Bobby that night, this trip wouldn't have been on—or not with us included. Peter would have brought Scott to get the new car, but they would have done it in the one day. Well, I'm going to make the most of this weekend, and if I haven't got Peter saying yes to the plans I have in mind by then my name isn't Jennifer.'

Victoria shook her head as she looked at the girl opposite. 'You're only eighteen, Jennifer——'

But, interrupting sharply, Jennifer said, 'I'm going on nineteen. . .well, in six months or so. And I know what I want!'

'Yes, you might think you do. But couldn't your mother and Peter be right? You *are* young, and you should give their plans some thought. . .'

'For heaven's sake, Victoria! I was at boarding-school for six years. I went out on all sorts of affairs in my senior terms—with all sorts of partners—and I mean all sorts of partners. So I realise how lucky I am with Peter, and I'm going to marry him, Mother and Peter notwithstanding!'

What could she say to that? thought Victoria, wishing she had the other girl's single-mindedness of purpose. But then she told herself not to be stupid. Scott wasn't Peter. Good heavens, she could just imagine herself trying to inveigle Scott into falling in with plans she had made. She shivered!

Jennifer had jumped up and was rummaging among the clothes in her overnight bag. She said, 'Come on, Victoria, we'll go and shower, then go and meet whatever the night brings to us.'

Victoria sighed. Oh, well, she'd play follow-the-leader and go to meet whatever the night brought for her too.

They ate dinner in an unexpectedly crowded dining-room, a large outback tourist bus having arrived to tour the caves. A tourist bus, moreover, with more than its share of youthful travellers, some of whom were showing a marked interest in their table.

Scott, of course, always drew glances, and tonight he could have stepped from the pages of a fashion spread. He looked as if he had never come in contact with dirty, crumpled riding clothes; never heard of a sweat-stained face.

Dressed in what looked like a raw silk, dark blue coat shirt worn outside trousers that matched, the colour lent to those eyes an even deeper shade, while above the smooth, tanned skin of his features the citrine hair glinted in the overhead lights.

Oh, well, tonight both she and Jennifer could also draw looks, she thought, her glance passing over one of the crowded tables of laughing, euphoric diners. She encounterd a gaze directed at her. She smiled in return, as she would have done in her student days, then allowed her glance to pass on. But, gazing down at her plate, Victoria gave a small secret smile. Tonight she merited that interested look. Worn for the first time, this dress was a Christmas present from her mother—and looked it. Created in lemon and white half-inch vertical stripes, it fell direct to her hips, where it bloused over a short straight skirt. And with its silken thinness outlining the upthrust pointed breasts, it was as modern as tomorrow.

'What's that complacent smile in aid of?' Scott was leaning close to speak to her, the warmth of his cheek reaching out to her own. Unable to help herself, she turned her head, and as blue eyes looked into grey that familiar cord, invisible yet steel-strong, fused them into stillness.

A waitress leaning down between them broke the current, and Scott moved sharply, pushing back his chair a little. Dinner was finishing, diners rising, and an exodus to the lounge began. A piano recital and dancing was being provided there for the tourists. They followed Jennifer and Peter, who were holding hands.

Victoria found she didn't have Scott all to herself from then on. He was in demand, and once, as she said thank you to a partner at the end of a dance, a glance towards the piano showed her a fair head hemmed in by a froth of vividly bright summer frocks, three deep.

She suddenly understood for the first time what Jennifer had said about him the day she had arrived up here. Yes, wherever he found himself, that magnetism, that aura which emanated from him would always draw the opposite sex to him. It wasn't fair, her mind said, as it had on other occasions.

However, she turned from that spectacle as Bobby pulled at her frock. 'I'm tired, Victoria,' his little piping treble told her, and gazing anxiously at him she noticed that he did look pale. Her quandary about what decision to make was solved for her. Moving to her side, Peter said, 'We're going for a walk to see the bluffs by moonlight, Victoria. Would you and Scott like to come too? Geoff can take Bobby up to bed.'

After a glance at that still laughing, hilarious group,

Victoria said, 'No, don't bother Scott. I'll take the boys upstairs. I don't think Bobby is too well.'

Peter might have demurred, but Jennifer didn't, and Victoria sighed as she watched their departing backs. She held out a hand, saying, 'Come along, love. Bed's the place for you.' She looked at Geoffrey and for once he didn't ask his eternal 'why?', only saying, 'OK, it's boring here anyway,' and walked along beside her.

Upstairs, she left them to get undressed and went to get an aspirin. Dissolving it, she told Bobby, 'Here you are, love,' and watched as he drank the lot. She folded clothes and tidied the room, then, seeing that Bobby's eyes were closed, waved goodnight to Geoffrey, switched out the lights and went next door.

There she changed into a nightdress, and smiled. It had lace on it, certainly, but it was no diaphanous chiffon affair that a girl going on a glamorous weekend would pack. Blue dimity cotton, it hung swinging from a yoke, and she looked like a little girl in it.

Absently she picked up her brush and drew it through her hair, wondering if Jennifer would be long, or if she should leave the light on for her. Then the brush in her hand went suddenly still. She turned slowly and looked at the man, not at his reflection.

She said, 'Bobby wasn't well, so I put him to bed with an aspirin. He's asleep now.'

'Yes, I know—I've just been in to see. Thank you, Victoria. I didn't realise you were gone.'

Suddenly, Victoria was grinning. 'No, I don't expect you did,' she told him.

And, laughing, Scott threw both hands upwards in acknowledgement. He said, 'They're visitors to our country; I was only showing them some of our far northern hospitality.'

Abruptly, a very different emotion was dancing in those sapphire eyes, and he walked a pace over the threshold to stand before her—so close, but not touching.

Then he took an extra step and a hand came round to rest against her back, bringing her to him. It moved up and down against the thin cotton of her nightdress, and her lids fell shut. She felt again, as she had in another bedroom, the jolt her heart gave as she was drawn into him, into the complete, hard curves of his entire body.

She heard his voice from above her say, 'I didn't mean to come here. I just called to check on Bobby. But fate seems to have had other ideas. . .and it doesn't do to disregard fate.'

Fingers came up to tilt her head back. She lay there on his arm, brown shining hair cascading in a waterfall across it; her face, herself, open to his wishes. As his lips came to rest on her own she knew that this kiss was different—premeditated, sensual.

She went to meet his desire with every nerve clamouring. . .remembering nothing, thinking of nothing but the hard demand that was reaching out to enfold her.

Then, bringing back reality, his lips moved from hers to rest for a moment by the corner of her mouth. 'Fate notwithstanding, I shouldn't be doing this,' he was murmuring, and in that silent, empty room only the sound of their quick breathing was audible.

Then Scott said what she had only been thinking. 'I organised this trip for my own purpose—to enable me to look at us both, calmly and coolly. However, I've had you with me all day, and all I've wanted to do is what I did a moment ago. That's not looking at things calmly and coolly. So for the rest of this trip you're going to be merely Geoffrey's teacher, and I'm just a friend saying thank you for helping me with Bobby.'

'But, Scott. . .' Feeling those lips resting so lightly beside her own, feeling the heaviness of his body against her, that hand still spread on her lower back, Victoria said again, 'But, Scott. . .'

'Look, Victoria, I can't just shrug off the way I've felt through a dozen years; the way I feel that you might decide later that living up here is not your scene——'

Suddenly she was furiously angry. 'Do you think. . .?' she asked him through clenched teeth. 'Do you think,' the words came repeated, 'that after knowing you I would ever think of leaving? You're being stupid, Scott, to equate one woman's views and desires with another's.'

As these fierce, wrathful words fell about them, abruptly the tension, the stress of emotion encircling them, shattered. White teeth gleamed in a bronzed face as Scott laughed down at her. 'Very well,' he said, 'I'll accept that there's an atttraction between us; that it might—could—be enough. . . However——' A long finger reached out to stroke down a cheek as he continued, 'Look, we'll leave it for now. Now isn't the time or place.' His glance swept around the room they were in and he repeated grimly, 'No, this is certainly not the place.'

Then Victoria wasn't thinking of mundane things like places. Scott was bending over her and saying, 'I have to go,' but the kiss he was bestowing upon her was one of intent, of promise. So she did what she could only do with him: she sent her body responding with no reserve whatever.

Then those hard worker's hands were standing her upright and he had swung away to depart with that lithe jungle tread of his, leaving no word, no other sound behind.

She stood there abandoned. She thought, I hate you, Scott Courtney—I really do! You're just not fair! She stared desolately out into the brilliant moonlit night, remembering that the world had surrounded them with the magic of beaten silver on that Einasleigh trip too— two months ago. She thought she would never like moonlight again.

Turning, she climbed into bed. She heard Jennifer and Peter talking as they came upstairs. She pulled the sheet high and turned her face to the wall, and pretended sleep when Jennifer spoke to her.

CHAPTER NINE

LAYERS of cotton wool were pressing against her face, smothering her. Frantically Victoria fought to push them aside—and sat up. Her opened eyes looked into anxious blue ones only inches away. Bobby withdrew the hand with which he had been patting her cheek, his glance turning suddenly apprehensive, and Victoria smiled.

'You gave me a fright, Bobby! What's the matter? Is your leg sore? Do you need something?'

'No. Only I was awake, and the others are still asleep. I thought you might like to go for a walk—I know you like to explore.'

'Do you indeed? OK, then, hop outside and give me five minutes to get dressed, and we'll go exploring. I'll have my second look at that bluff—even if it is only in daylight.'

She dressed quickly, and they crept hand in hand through a hotel that was just beginning to go about its business of welcoming a new day. Outside, Victoria raised her face to the fresh sparkling morning and smiled at her small companion.

Today the bluff held no magic. Bathed in golden sunshine, it was only a prosaic giant hill of large granite rocks. 'Let's go up a little way,' Bobby was entreating, pulling at her hand.

'Good heavens, no! You might slip.' She shuddered at the very idea of taking him back to his guardian, hurt again. So they sauntered along, Bobby kicking his toes in the stony ground and finding his own kind of treasures.

Finally they retraced their steps to the hotel, where, seeing his cousin filling the new Rover with petrol, Bobby let go of her hand and ran across to him. Victoria stood undecided, then shrugged and turned to enter the open doorway.

'Oh, good, Victoria!' exclaimed Jennifer. 'Peter said to tell you to bring your gear down when you come to breakfast. We're booked on the first tour of the caves, and we'll go straight home from there.'

Victoria gazed at the white pleated skirt and navy blouse-topped frock which she had unpacked, and shrugged, dismissing the jeans beside it. Jeans might be the garment to wear, but this was a special outing for her, and the dress would allow freedom of movement and coolness. So, donning it and the sensible white and navy trimmed walking shoes that matched it, she used foundation and lipstick, finished her packing, then told the serious grey eyes framed in folds of shining hair, 'Well, here we go!' and picked up her case.

Peter was emerging from the bar, Scott from the open doorway. 'Everything's fixed this end, mate,' said Peter, 'and as long as that new toy of yours is ready and checked, we can be off.'

He grinned widely across at Scott, the smile showing that everything in Peter's world at this moment was exactly where he wanted it to be.

'It's as ready as it will ever be,' came the dry reply. Then the speaker turned and saw her. He said, 'Good morning, Victoria.'

She looked back at him and replied carefully with the same two words he had used, then went before the two men into the dining-room.

Later, on their way, gazing at an interstate number plate on the vehicle before them, Bobby asked, 'How far away is Victoria, Victoria? And were you called after an Australian state?' He was giggling at his own cleverness.

'I shouldn't imagine I was, little sticky-beak. As for how far away that southern state is, my geography is pretty rusty, but I would think Victoria could be three thousand miles or so away.' The number plate they were discussing was turning off the main road, so following it, Scott edged their own vehicle into a shaded clearing.

'Are we there?' Bobby's small voice floated upwards.

'Yes.' The monosyllable came from his cousin.

Victoria gazed about her at this place she had heard so much about it. It was like the bluff she had seen in Chillagoe, but so very much larger. A mountain of granite, it stretched away on both sides, and looked age-old, unchanged since the beginning of time.

A big iron grille faced them, securing an opening. Their guide swung the framework of crossed bars wide, and Victoria gazed a little apprehensively into the gaping vault beyond. Blackness before had only been a relative sensation. She had never experienced Stygian darkness.

'What kind of lights are those?' she asked, throwing out an enquiring hand to where unfamiliar lights were being ignited with little spurts of sound.

'Carbide,' answered Peter, leaving her none the wiser.

Scott was addressing the boys. 'Now don't go fooling around in there,' she heard him say. 'Half of these caves have never been explored, and I don't want to go home leaving someone behind.'

They stepped into velvet blackness pierced by only those two pinpoints of brilliance. They trod along galleries, hanging on to what seemed to Victoria the frailest of handrails. They stood in a vast cavern, gazing with awe about them; at enormous stalagmites and stalactites, glittering. . .scintillating. It was thrilling. It was an unknown experience, but it was a bit frightening too, this huge incredible place in the very bowels of the earth.

'I hope to goodness they know their way around!' Victoria heard the man in front of her say.

'I'll drink to that,' she muttered, not intending to be facetious at all.

Then, with only a bare announcement, the lights they had come to regard as the link with the world they knew went out. Victoria knew Scott was beside her, but merely knowing brought no reassurance. She put out a hand to touch his shirt-clad shoulder, thankful for the solidness of it. Then, as swiftly as they had been plunged into blackness, light was with them again, brilliant, ablaze.

'Behold the ballroom!' said their guide.

It *was* like a ballroom, staged and coloured and hung with curtains of draped, petrified stone.

All too soon the big lights were switched off, and they were following their carbide illumination once more. 'Where's Bobby?' Victoria looked uneasily round the group.

'Geoff's got him, he's all right.' Scott's answer was placid.

Suddenly Victoria gave a gurgle of laughter. She was looking at the image in rough, petrified stone of a head that could have been Winston Churchill's. It didn't even need the cigar with which someone had embellished it. The likeness was uncanny.

Admiring it too long, hurrying to catch up with light already getting dimmer, she spoke breathlessly. 'Scott, Bobby has just gone off that offshoot there. I saw him disappearing. . .'

'Of course you didn't, Victoria. He's with Geoff, I told you.' Scott was trying to hurry her along more quickly.

'No, I did see. . .' she was beginning, when abruptly only a vault of darkness was crowding them in. The rest of their party had turned a corner.

Panicking, she took two hurried paces to where she thought Scott would be, and kicked against a projecting stone. Falling headlong, she lay gasping, the breath knocked from her. A hand slid across her prostrate body, and with her mouth opened to scream she felt fingers close over it.

'Be quiet while we listen.' Scott's whisper was the merest sound as he leant above her. She shook her head and the fingers lifted, but no comforting sound of a guide's voice calling came to them.

'Don't move,' continued that casual, easy voice. 'They count all the time; they must have found we're missing. But we must stay exactly where we are, Victoria. I don't know if the wall is behind us or before us, so we'll just sit down here. Would it be too much to expect that you have a lighter or matches?'

'Yes, it would be. No, I haven't!' She tried to make herself speak as easily as her companion had done.

'You know,' came the disembodied voice from beside her, 'I always carry matches—I might need them at any time in the bush. But today, hurrying, I didn't expect to want them. Serves me right. . .' The words broke off.

A hand came out to move over her until it reached an arm. He said, 'I've patted all round here and it's flat, so come close.' Victoria found herself drawn tightly against his side, then felt the other hand doing its turn of patting over her—an absolutely impersonal hand—to find her lower limbs and bring them also into what Scott considered safety. The fingers came to rest on a thigh, bare and smooth. Dresses while exploring caves *did* have some disadvantages!

She felt that silent, familiar ripple run through him,
and he said, amusement colouring the soft voice, 'I must
say, Victoria, you pick the weirdest places! Are you by
any chance, my grey-eyed siren, trying to seduce me in
this place, in this river of the night?'

'I might just be thinking of it, if it weren't so
uncomfortable, and I weren't so frightened,' she retorted,
with no sign of love or romance in words that were more
than a little breathless.

Abruptly all facetiousness had gone, and even in the
Stygian blackness Victoria could discern the change in
his voice. He was saying carefully, 'Let's leave all that
for now. OK?'

'Yes.' She was quite ready to leave it—for now! So, in
his arms, kept safe from the frightening blackness encircling them, she held on to the fingers entwined firmly
about her own. She did ask, when what seemed as if an
aeon had passed, but what was possibly only seconds,
'They *will* come, won't they?'

'Of course they will. Don't be silly, Victoria.' Cold,
authoritative, these words stopped the words she had
been about to utter. But then, almost at once, Scott was
continuing, 'They're coming now, I think.'

It seemed that was the case, because, imperceptibly at
first, but swiftly getting stronger, the darkness around
them was lifting. Then a sigh of thankfulness went
through her as a 'cooee' came towards them through the
deep silence.

It was not loud yet, but it echoed all round. Then the
call came again, and, answering it, Scott set her a small
distance away from him.

Using a placatory tone to the solitary guide who had
come to stand beside them, Scott was saying, 'I'm sorry.
We stayed too long looking at the Churchill face, then

Miss Steene fell over that big lump of rock there—and all of a sudden you seemed to have disappeared. I thought it best to stay exactly where we were until you returned for us.'

'That's all very well, Mr Courtney,' their rescuer was beginning, still sounding angry. 'But it could have ended——'

'I realise that, and I have apologised,' Scott's voice, clipped, assured, was answering. 'We should have kept up with you; the fault is mine. Look, can we get along? Miss Steene is very cold.'

Yes, they could get along, when asked in that tone.

'Is my little cousin with you?' her companion was asking pleasantly as they followed the light. 'Miss Steene thought she saw him leave the party. I'm quite sure, however, she must have been mistaken.'

'No, she wasn't! That flipping Leith kid knew about that side passage we use sometimes to amuse the tourists; there's no danger in it, you only have to slide between very narrow walls. It's a short cut, and the kids were waiting for us when we entered the sky cave. He was told off, I can tell you! We can't have that sort of thing in the caves. That, I expect, was probably the reason we didn't miss you two as quickly as we might have done. My partner took the others out and I came back for you.'

Emerging blinking into the late morning sunshine, Peter grinned at them, saying, 'Half your luck, mate. Why didn't I think of that?'

'Because you're not me, mate. From all the tales circulating around me up here, you should know I have my own way of doing things.' Scott was grinning at his friend, but these easy, laughing words placed the small episode where it belonged—behind them.

In minutes they were in the Land Rover and taking off

for home, and from where he was resting against Victoria's side Bobby's voice came sleepily. 'It's been a beaut weekend, hasn't it, Scott? But it'll be nice to get home to Shad and Old Bill.'

Noting the contentment in his tone, Victoria looked down and saw that he was asleep—just like that. What it was to be a child!

'Scott?' She nerved herself to speak. 'Scott,' she asked, 'what's really going to happen about us?'

The driver took his glance from the winding track for a brief moment to look down. Victoria caught her breath. Never before had she seen him look like that. She realised suddenly why he was talked about in the way he was, the reputation he had!

One brow had unexpectedly lifted, and those sapphire eyes weren't dense, impenetrable now. They were pirate's eyes, looking over a captive with diamond pinpoints that glittered.

'What was the question you asked, Victoria? Was it something like, what about us? But I told you back there in—what did I call it then?—that river of the night, that we'd leave serious discussion of our dilemma for now. However. . .however, there are always alternatives!

'For instance, there are such things as temporary affairs. Now there's a suggestion. Would you be interested in a temporary affair with me, Victoria? We'd have the whole bush as a playground. And whatever else I am or am not, I certainly am a bushman. We wouldn't get lost, no matter where we roamed or came to pause. Then in a couple of years, if you decided this wasn't your scene, you could leave it all behind you. Now, how about that?'

Victoria's held-in breath exhaled, but her hands, out of sight, were clasped tightly together. How was she to answer him? She remembered that look of Scott's just now—but she also remembered other times. The way he had knelt in the dirt to rub away an agonising cramp; the tenderness he had used to her in the caves when she had been so frightened. And this she knew too: the times he could have started an affair with her, and hadn't.

How was she to reply? She knew that sometimes she didn't know how to take him. Then, deliberately, defiantly straightening her back, she drew a deep breath and said, 'Very well, then, Scott. With my upbringing, I would prefer orange blossom, lace and white satin, with a choir singing in church. However, I'll take what you offer, bushland playground and all. I accept!'

'Oh!' the violent ejaculation was forced from her involuntarily. The Land Rover had been driven deliberately over a large rock on the side of the road. Victoria flew up, her head almost hitting the roof. 'You did that on purpose, Scott!' she exclaimed wrathfully.

'Yes, I *did* do it in purpose. I don't want to hear you speak like that again. Do you understand me?'

Oh, yes, she understood him! She also hated him! She turned her face away and put up a hand to rub away tears with the back of her wrist.

She heard muttered words from under her breath, and suddenly Scott had pulled the Rover to a stop.

'Victoria,' he said.

She didn't answer, she didn't turn round, and across Bobby's sleeping form he reached out a hand. So, turning because she had to, she said fiercely, 'I hate you!'

Then he smiled at her, and the gentleness of it brought the tears surging again. He told her, and his tone matched that unknown smile, 'You probably do, but you'd better use a tissue, because we're stopping for lunch.' He swung the vehicle into motion and was soon following Peter into a clearing at the side of the road.

Still apprehensive about the furore his little trick in the caves had caused, Geoffrey kept well away from the adults and charged about gathering wood, eagerly building a fire. Jennifer was helping, while Victoria attended to a just awakened Bobby.

'Here you are, Victoria, lunch fit for the gods from our five-star hotel, corned beef and pickle sandwiches.' Peter was holding out a greaseproof-wrapped package.

She took it and smiled at him. One could always smile at Peter. There were no undercurrents where he was concerned. She also accepted the enamel mug from Geoffrey, giving him a small smile too.

'Thanks, Victoria,' he replied, and she knew what that thank-you was for. He was in real trouble from everyone.

She sipped the tea, then drank it all—this billy tea which held a tang so unlike any other she had tasted. She ate what food she could manage; she laughed with Peter and talked with Jennifer, she coaxed Bobby to eat his lunch.

And there, across from her, leaning indolently in his own particular style against a big tree, was the man she sometimes hated, and sometimes. . . She turned quickly away to look elsewhere.

They got on with their alfresco meal, and when they had finished Peter carefully stamped out the fire; Scott was walking over to swing Bobby high to deposit him in the back of the Rover.

Opening the front door for her, he said, 'Do I need to says ups-a-daisy to you and swing you up too? No, I don't expect I do,' and only held out a hand to enable her to step decorously into the high passenger seat.

For five minutes or so there was only silence in the

small cabin as they drove along. Scott glanced backwards over his shoulder at Bobby, but seeing him watching out of his window to look for the familiar landscape of home appearing brought his gaze back and said, 'I have to go away for a week or ten days, up to the Gulf with Shad——'

'Why tell me? What is it to me where you go?' Bitterness coloured the words. Then she was continuing, 'It's all the same to me if you're up in the Gulf or down here at home from now on. I'm going to be busy with Geoffrey. Getting him into college is one thing I'm going to succeed in doing.'

'Yes, well. . .' Scott took his gaze off the road to glance around at her before continuing, and for the second time she saw that those dense sapphire eyes had that piratical, dancing look emanating from them as he told her, 'Shad and I are working on a little surprise—and being away up in the Gulf is part of it. Accept that it's the way I feel about you, that I'm even mentioning it to you, Victoria, because we're preparing for the Einasleigh Races, and we don't want the least little glimmer of it to get out. Not to anyone! And that includes Peter and the Hamiltons as well. So, my houri of that river of darkness back there, you have my complete trust, even if. . .' The words broke off and he said, 'Victoria!'

She turned to look at him. Allowing the Rover to slow, Scott reached out a hand. Tanned brown fingers came to rest on her temples, then lightly trailed down her cheek to continue on their journey. Sliding slowly over bare apricot skin, they left in their wake every nerve clamouring; this seductive, tenuous caress that set her pulses jumping, that sent her body melting towards him.

Head thrown back, she yet saw those fingers take hold of her hand, prise it open and drop within it a kiss as

light as his touch had been. She shivered, and closed it
into a fist. The Land Rover abruptly surged forward,
gravel and small stones scattering. And Bobby called out,
'We're home!'

They *were* home—well, at Scott's home. And Shad
was there smiling as he opened the door to help her
down. Victoria sat still for a moment gazing down at the
dark man; this almost brother, everyone said, of the man
she loved. He looked up and as he encountered the
expression her glance held his own swung abruptly
sideways to where Scott had come to stand beside him,
his eyes questioning. They flickered, then he was again
his usual quiet, distant self.

She put her hand into his and stepped down, and
heard Old Bill ask, 'Did you like my brownie, missy?'

'Indeed I did. It was just the thing for morning tea in
the bush,' she answered.

He cackled delightedly, and as Bobby came to stand
with him she smiled at all of them—all three of Scott
Courtney's possessions. She flipped a hand and walked
across to their own vehicle.

From its haven, she gazed over what could have been
a theatre backdrop, with the old colonial house silhouetted in the crimson afterglow of a disappearing sun. Peter
started their car.

Twilight came running to meet them, then departed.
And suddenly there was only darkness, with a blazing
Southern Cross riding high in the heavens.

Pleading tiredness, Victoria went to her room after
they had eaten, and in bed thought of the man who had
brought laughter to that dark nightmare of the caves. . .
And Scott was suddenly in the room, his arms holding
her; then his look had changed abruptly and she saw him
laughing at her while offering an affair. She twisted

restlessly, for most of all she was remembering that exquisite, tender caress in the Land Rover just before they arrived home.

The slow hours passed and, unable to sleep, she got up, and going to the bathroom took two aspirins from the packet, swallowing them down with a glass of water. She returned to bed, determined to sleep.

She found that trying not to think of Scott didn't help, so she gave herself up to remembering, thinking of him. And when eventually oblivion did come to claim her, she found she was enfolded not in darkness but in the cushioned safety of strong encircling arms.

CHAPTER TEN

LIFE settled back into a routine, and in the schoolroom they were working hard. Victoria, pushing extraneous subjects from her mind, was trying to get Geoffrey ready for that entrance exam which was the reason for her presence here.

'We're going to the extension, Victoria, we're all needed,' said Mrs Leith one morning, coming into the room. 'Geoff must come, and you can if you want to. But don't think you'll be going on another picnic. Today will be work, and you'll come home filthy and covered with dust.'

'The extension—that's at Namangilla, isn't it, where those swamps are?'

'Yes. Our stock tends to drift that way because of the greener grass around them. Pete says there's a muster going on and we'd better go and collect ours before someone else does.'

'I'd like to go, and what's a bit of dust and hard riding between friends?' smiled Victoria.

'You'll get more than a bit of both,' she was answered drily, then Mrs Leith departed, saying over her shoulder, 'Hurry up, both of you!'

Yes, she would hurry up, thought Victoria. She would make an extra effort for anything to do with Namangilla and its owner. She flew to her room to climb into jeans, a long-sleeved shirt, and a wide-brimmed hat. She was outside waiting when Geoffrey brought the horses to the front gate.

Their leisurely canter ate up the miles, and when the green smudge came into view on the horizon Victoria felt a stir of excitement. There were the swamps she had heard so much about.

'Are those swamps really dangerous, Mrs Leith? I mean, could anyone wander into them and get hurt. . .or lost?'

'Indeed they are dangerous, and people up here know that. I expect only Scott and Shad know their way through them, and the Aboriginals, of course.'

A lowing of cattle, then a cloud of dust haze, came wafting along to meet them, and Jack, riding in his cattleman's lope, accosted the older woman. 'Mr Brown said for you to ride this mob, Mrs Leith. They're ours and he wants them to stay that way.' Jack gave a wide white-toothed smile, then turned to lope away on his own little jobs.

Victoria found she had no time to wonder where a certain person was. She also found, as she had been warned, that she was not at a picnic outing.

She rode a horse that twisted and turned; she eased reluctant stock back into their mob. Then unexpectedly, abruptly, in a split second, she discovered that the lazy, hazy day about her had changed. Out of the churning mob, a half-grown steer, wild, violence in every thrusting muscle, charged straight for her group. A horseman, dark, sweat-stained, sent a rope flashing. There came a slither of hooves and both steer and rider were held together by a slender twist of jute. Lowering its head, the brute charged this new harassment.

Then a second horseman, filthy and dust-begrimed too, but whose matted hair glinted golden in front of the big hat, sent a rope flickering. The animal, held by two stretched ropes, was taken well away from the branding area. It had been an exercise in flawlessness between the two men, Victoria thought, as she urged her mount from behind her mob to which she had sidled out of harm's way. But still the golden horseman kept away from her vicinity.

At smoko-time she found herself a place well away from where they were branding; that was the one aspect of today she didn't like. Eating with Bobby, who had come to sit beside her, she asked, 'Do you think we could go and have a look at the swamp, Bobby? I'd really like to.'

The small boy finished his sandwich, throwing the crusts to a crow which was watching them intently with a beady eye. It hopped to snatch its prize, sunlight sheening the ebony of its plumage. Bobby's reply was a little reluctant.

'We can go and look, I suppose. But we mustn't go in.'

So, moving to her waiting horse, Victoria tightened the girth and, setting foot in the stirrup, swung easily into the saddle. She felt the sun-warmed leather creak as she settled into it, and thought absently on hearing the sound, I do love this country. It *is* where I want to be. Why can't Scott understand that?

They left the bawling cattle behind; they still took with them a sky tinted a hazy lapis lazuli, and a burning sun that poured its heat over the whole land. Arriving at the edge of the swamp, Victoria urged her horse slowly forward. It didn't seem at all dangerous. It looked lovely and green and cool.

A small brown hand on her rein swung her gaze sideways. 'Not too far, Victoria,' said her little companion. 'Scott would be wild!'

'Oh, I won't go in far. But I'd like to see in there where it looks so green. I'll go carefully.'

Her knees prodded the little horse and it paced a few more steps, putting its feet down delicately as if picking a way it didn't like. The ground remained firm, the emerald-green grass clumps becoming more interwoven. Edging further in, she saw the creepers, the completely unknown ferns and strange plants. She thought the whole place beautiful and went to move closer to see more of it.

'Come back, Victoria!' Bobby was calling urgently, and suddenly she became aware that the satin muscles between her legs were quivering, rippling and trembling as her mount stood absolutely still.

Frightened now, fully intending to go back, she pulled at the reins, trying to turn. The horse took one reluctant step sideways and halted. Victoria heard a sucking sound, and the animal beneath her jerked convulsively. She found herself banged against a creeper-laden tree from which something detached itself and twined about her. She cried out, thrusting violently at it, almost falling.

'Keep perfectly still,' said Scott's voice from below her. She obeyed, deathly afraid now. The sucking sound was louder and she knew she had acted with criminal stupidity.

'Pull back on the reins—hard! Do as you're bloody told!' The shouted words penetrated, and she pulled with all her strength. Beneath her, Scott's hands were straining on the offside front leg, which was already disappearing. He was pulling; she could see the corded ridge of muscle outlined under the tanned skin.

The little mare's head was almost in her lap, its mane all over her, the shoulder muscles tense with straining. We're not going to make it, she thought desperately. But the prayer she was muttering was for the man as he worked down there in that thick green slime.

Flung backwards on her mount's rump as it reared loose, Victoria clung tightly. It wasn't as stupid as she had been. It backed carefully, as if treading on eggshells it didn't want to break.

Then both of them were standing on firm ground, and she saw long, entangling lengths of slimy creeper still clinging to her.

Shaking, she could only remain quiet in the saddle, immobile, shock keeping her silent and unable to move. She was lifted down and she stood leaning helplessly against her mount. Scott detached the vine and heaved it back into its own habitat. He had spoken no word except for that first violent outburst. Then he turned to Bobby.

'Go back—quietly, now, mate. There's no need to talk about this. You understand?'

Bobby understood, hearing that tone in his cousin's voice. He glanced from her to Scott, and she saw that both masculine faces were showing no colour under a tan which was almost grey. Then Bobby had turned obediently and eased his horse towards the busy scene where branding had been resumed.

'For heaven's sake, Victoria, haven't you any sense! You must have been told about this place—and there are warning signs. . .' No love, no protective gesture flowed her way this time as it had once done in another frightening situation. Only deep anger showed, which a voice kept low made worse.

'I know I was stupid, Scott, and I am sorry, but I did go in only a little way. Ugh!' Shuddering, she pulled away another piece of thick vine still clinging to her, while saying, 'It's like a snake—horrible!' She was trying shakily to speak lightly of what had just happened.

'It could just as well have been a snake! Hell, you need a horsewhip around your shoulders for risking not only your own life but your mount's as well! You could have been killed, sucked into that quagmire. . .and your horse certainly would have been even if we'd saved you!'

'I'm sorry. . . I am! Please don't look at me like that.'

'Just how should I look at you?' answered this stranger standing before her, granite-faced. Those eyes she knew so well were staring at her from an inimical countenance caked with perspiration and dust. 'You could have been killed,' he said again, and the words reached out to her, ice-cold and cutting. 'But no, I don't expect that would have happened. Shad was watching and we both know this place—but if anyone else had had to try to get you out, we'd have had a tragedy on our hands.'

He said again, and this time she noticed under cold, arctic words a far-back tremble, 'How could you have done such a dangerous, senseless thing, Victoria? You must have been told about this place!'

'I was—Mrs Leith told me. I'm sorry, Scott.' Her hand went out entreatingly, but it was ignored. Then abruptly that blistering tone changed. It spoke in the way she had once heard it speak in a safe, comfortable kitchen. It said in a soft silken cadence threaded through with filaments of stretched steel,

'Do you know, Victoria, that I want you more than I've ever wanted any woman—in all sorts of ways? I'd even begun to wonder if, in spite of past experience, something could be worked out. But, thank heaven, this little escapade has brought me to my senses. No girl from up here would ever do such a thing; and now, at this moment, I realise how many other things could go wrong.

'So while you're up here you'll be to me merely Mrs Leith's guest.' He added what she herself had said twice,

'I'm sorry, Victoria. Believe me, for myself too! Here, I'll give you a leg up.' Finality coloured the last sentence.

She still stood unmoving, her legs unable to obey the command her brain was sending to them. But what else could she do or say? Scott meant what he had just said; you could see it in every line of his entire face and body. She thought desolately that if he really wanted to spoil their lives for just one stupid thing she had done. . .well, so be it!

She made herself move a couple of steps to the side of the little horse, and Scott's fingers gripped her elbow as she went to step into the stirrup—and missed. Then her foot had found the iron support and, with that hard hand helping her, she found herself in the saddle. She gathered up the reins and with her head held as high as she could manage walked her mount away, not even turning her head as she heard that other horse and rider loping off in the opposite direction.

Back on the outskirts of their own stock, she saw that the work was going on as usual, and that fortunately no one seemed to have noticed what had happened. Then, unable to help herself, Victoria sent one swift backward glance over her shoulder to where the owner of this station was checking along the edges of the swamp, making sure no stock was near it—or in it.

She saw a small herd of animals being urged along by two riders, and, not knowing them, only trying to bring back some normality into her metabolism, she asked Geoffrey who they were.

'Oh, they're stockmen from the Lagoons station way up in the Gulf,' he told her. 'They have a long way to go, so we've cut out their stock first. But we won't be long here either.'

They weren't, and Victoria took the place Uncle Pete

indicated beside their own mob. She didn't look round for Scott! She rode beside the slowly moving cattle, then turned to look sideways as a horse nudged up beside her own. Glancing upwards, she gazed into Shad's eyes.

She said, 'I'm sorry for what I did! I really didn't realise it could be so dangerous as I was close beside the edge.'

'It isn't in a lot of places. You just picked a bad one, and I don't suppose you did realise that what you were doing put both you and your mount into danger. The swamps can be very deceptive. But, for now, will you take some advice from me, Victoria?'

'Of course I will.'

Shad smiled, answering in that slow voice of his, 'Don't you want to know the advice?'

Victoria shook her head. 'Not from you, if it's about Scott,' she answered.

'Well, then, I suggest you just go along with the way things are, and we'll see what the future brings. It was the shock of seeing you in that quicksand that brought on Scott's anger. You really were in danger, you know. However. . .' Again a smile lit up the dark face as he said, 'We have a few little things going for us—like the Einasleigh Races, for instance—and if we can't come up with something between us I don't deserve to have known Scott all my life. We'll see.' A hand waved, a horse dropped back, and Victoria was riding by herself again.

As she thought of Shad's comforting words, the heavy load of depression that had engulfed her lifted a little and she straightened in her saddle and began, like the other riders, to urge the animals around them to move more quickly to their own home ground.

So she waited the days out; she got on with her own job and heard talk about the Einasleigh Races—and

didn't even ask one question. Jennifer had had a new
dress sent up for the Race Ball, and when it came she
tried it on, dancing up and down the long room.

As she watched her, the thought went through Victoria's
mind that she was so lucky. Everything was going right
for her the first time she fell in love. Jennifer's mother
might want a more advantageous marriage for her, seeing
what the girl would inherit. But this girl knew what she
wanted, and Peter would make a wonderful husband.
Lucky both of you, Victoria thought.

Finally, the day they were waiting for came along, and
they were off to Einasleigh. Across the river, the world
was beginning to take on shape through a haze of grey
mist that was the forerunner to daybreak when a voice
greeting Mrs Leith made Victoria swing round.

Scott! She couldn't believe it! His name had never
been mentioned amid all the frenetic preparations for this
trip.

She saw him accept a beaker of tea, then lean back
against a bench to direct his ironic smile at Jennifer. 'Too
bad, little one,' he told her, 'that you'll have to put up
with me. I'm afraid Peter's transporting the mission
crowd.'

'Don't put on a turn, Jennifer!' exclaimed her mother
as the girl turned on her. 'We thought it was practical
that they go straight to Einasleigh from the mission.
Everyone has to fit in with transport up here—you know
that!'

'Things seem to work out the way you want them, just
the same,' replied her daughter indignantly, stalking out
through the kitchen.

From under downcast lashes, Victoria gazed at the
figure leaning indolently on a bench, then returned to her
tea and the view across the river. Shafts of colour were

beginning to shoot from the horizon to brighten into a sea of scarlet and crimson; to the delicacy of gold and saffron, then to the palest yellow.

Then, as suddenly as they had arrived, the mists of the rainbow were gone—only a huge orb of gold remained, emerging piece by piece over the edge of the world.

'Where's your case, Victoria?' called Scott's voice from across the big room as naturally as if he had never spoken to her as he had done beside those horrible swamps. 'You and Jennifer and the two boys are to come with me. Pete and Mrs Leith are picking up the Paxtons in the Jaguar.'

Victoria pointed to her case, and wondered. With Scott, she knew, transport would be adapted to suit his requirements, even if normally it *was* organised to fit around far-flung localities.

She shrugged, dismissing any wondering about the reason why he was driving them. She would take what the gods provided and enjoy what she had never expected—Scott's undiluted company for over two hours on the road to Einasleigh.

And it must be his willing company! She simply couldn't imagine him being shanghaied into any situation, any schedule in which he didn't want to be included, transportation problems or no. So she followed her case and the man carrying it out to his Rover. Here, Jennifer informed him brusquely, 'I'll ride in the back.'

Scott shrugged, then asked, 'What about you, Victoria? Do you want to ride in the back too?'

'Wherever I fit in, thank you.' She was carefully polite—a guest accepting a lift.

And sitting in the front passenger seat, waiting for the big car up front to move off, she glanced quickly at this man she had not seen since he had been so angry with her. She had thought of him, oh, yes, of course. . . She had also thought of Shad, and the advice he had given her. She *had* just let time slide by—waiting. What other choice had she had?

His look scanning the instrument panel, Scott's down-bent face was sun-glazed and smooth. Tiny white lines radiating from the corners of his eyes were the only thing to break the symmetry of even, polished bronze. Those eyes of turquoise blue lifted unexpectedly.

'Inspection over?' asked their owner.

Victoria felt a rush of colour tint her throat and cheeks, but made herself say calmly, 'Was I staring? I'm sorry,' and swung her glance to her own window.

The road they were travelling this morning was of course not familiar, even if she had been on it once before—and had had the same driver. That journey had occurred at night-time and she had been thinking of nothing but a hurt little boy.

The big car before them was turning into a side-road, and Scott said, 'I'll move along. They won't want to be travelling in our dust when they come out again.' After that he drove in silence, and Victoria was quiet too, only answering when spoken to from the back.

Before long they were swinging past what seemed a settlement of tents. Surely this wasn't Einasleigh? It looked like a temporary army camp. But soon signs of civilisation did begin to come into view. Actually, it was not much bigger than Chillagoe. However, today of course there were people everywhere. . .and horses and vehicles of every description.

Jennifer and the boys flew down from the back almost before they had stopped. Shad was there, accompanied by a pretty dark girl, and he smiled his slow smile at Victoria as he helped her down. There were also two young men walking towards them, tall, fair, white teeth

flashing in suntanned smiling faces; assurance an aura
they carried with them. Too flawless altogether, thought
Victoria, who had seen others like them at university.
She wondered what might be the defect. Self-esteem,
conceit. . .

However, she found it was not conceit. They spied
Shad, and made for him as if pulled by one string,
pummelling his shoulder and slapping him wherever they
could reach as he fended them off. She saw friendship on
all three of their faces—and then on a fourth as Scott
joined them. Then the latecomer was looking directly
across into her eyes.

'Come and be introduced!' he called, and with that
ironical smile he sometimes used he told her, 'John and
Jamie Hamilton, Victoria. If you like this country up
here, grab! They own nearly half of it. Shad and I worked
for their father once upon a time.'

'Worked is hardly the operative word, Scott,' one of
the twins said. 'You ran that station as you saw fit, and,'
he turned to Victoria, 'under him we learnt how to run
cattle, because if we didn't learn it the easy way, there
was always the hard one.'

Scott grinned, and Shad laughed softly, but knowing
Scott by now, and all his moods, Victoria sensed that he
was only absently taking part in this give and take; his
attention was elsewhere.

A tall, fair elderly man was moving towards them with
a cattleman's walk. He asked the two men, one so fair,
the other dark, facing his sons, 'Who's going to win
today? Or must we wait until the race is run to find out?
We'll just have to finish this hold you two have on the
big race.'

'Today could very well be that time, Mr Hamilton,'
Scott told him, and Victoria noticed the deference in his

tone—the first time she had heard such an expression
colour it. 'I'm not racing. Only Shad is carrying our
colours—we suddenly found we only had one horse well
and healthy. We did wonder if anyone had been wandering around Namangilla in the dark. It was only just a
wonder, you know. . .' He broke off, grinning, as the
insults began flying his way.

'Aren't you really riding, Scott?' asked one of the
twins.

'No, not today. I have other fish to fry. Fancy taking
yourself away riding when you can. . .' He broke off
with his gaze wandering over the crowd, stopping at
every pretty girl as it passed. He laughed at the comments
he received, and waving a hand said, 'I'm off to attend to
my other fish.'

They settled in, and, with Jennifer off somewhere with
Peter, Victoria leaned against a veranda railing gazing at
the busy scene outspread before her. She saw Scott, and
a hundred other young men—and with a stab of the heart
she also saw the beautiful Joanna. So she had returned—
if only for this glamorous occasion. Victoria hoped it *was*
only for a glamorous occasion, because she was certainly
beautiful.

Returning her employer's smile as the older woman
came out to stand beside her, Victoria noticed her glance
follow one of the Hamilton twins as he walked past. She
could read the expression on Mrs Leith's face. Victoria
shrugged. Jennifer had known these boys all her life, and
if all she could do was just send a casual 'Hi' in their
direction, then it wasn't any use a mother gazing after
one of them with frustration in her glance. Attraction
found strange bedfellows. Hadn't she herself reason to
know that?

The dining-room was crowded when they went in for lunch. Victoria ate what was placed before her, and glanced round for one special familiar face. It wasn't there. Neither was Shad's.

CHAPTER ELEVEN

VICTORIA went to the Races; she gave a good exhibition of enjoying herself. She looked everywhere for a man who didn't seem to be there.

Then, beside the racecourse railing, watching the horses walk past to the starting-post for the big race that everyone was here for, her body went suddenly still. Scott's face was so close she could have put out a hand and stroked with her fingers along a satin-smooth tanned cheek.

He was standing beside a little black horse which Shad was riding, and although the fence of the racecourse ran between only inches separated their two figures. It wasn't fair, she thought as she had done so many times before, that he had all that he did have going for him—good looks, assurance, and a charisma that coloured the air-waves all about him. And also, honesty compelled her to add, a kindness that came through in all sorts of odd ways.

Then, as if another sort of wavelength had caught at his attention, Scott's head turned sharply. As that dense blue gaze met hers his eyes flew wide. For the space of a heartbeat their two forms were locked together, invisibly held by a stretched tension flowing between them.

He hadn't expected this meeting, she suddenly realised, and wasn't prepared for it. The expression in those sapphire eyes told her that. Then the lids fell and only a smooth, bronzed profile was presented to her.

Jamie Hamilton, riding a gleaming chestnut thoroughbred, had joined them. He looked the two men over, one
riding, one standing by holding a rein.

'I didn't expect the day would ever come,' he
exclaimed, 'when only one of you would be riding in the
big race!' Then abruptly he sent a raking glance over the
small animal beneath Shad. His mouth turned down.
'That's not one of your own horses. Where are they?'
The last question came sharply.

'Oh, come on, Jamie!' It was Scott's voice answering
gently. 'You can't expect peasants like us to have the
thoroughbreds a station like yours can come up with. *We*
have to do with the brumbies we can find.'

Victoria thought Jamie would have apoplexy by the
congestion on his face, by his effort of trying to force all
the words he could think of out at once. Before he could
get more than a few chosen expletives out, his brother
had cantered up. He too looked the small black, ung-
roomed horse over, saying as Jamie had, 'I don't believe
it! That you're riding that thing, Shad. . .' But before he
could say more, there came a flurry of movement as the
horses moved to the starting-post. Scott disappeared
under the rails.

Uncle Pete said, 'I expect I'm stupid, backing against
Namangilla, but my money's going on Mapleton's grey.
How about you?' he asked Mrs Leith

She handed him ten dollars. 'On Shad, of course. I'm
not stupid!'

'But really—that thing with its hangdog air! I don't
know what's come over them both.'

'Pete, who is the best rider in the territory?' asked Mrs
Leith curtly.

The iron-grey head turned to look at her. 'Oh, well,'
he said, 'I expect Scott is. . .or Shad, but still——'

'You've known them both all their lives. Do you think Shad would get out there before all this crowd,' Mrs Leith's arm swung round in a throwaway gesture, 'and ride something that ran like a packhorse? I don't say he might not lose—that could happen to anybody, in any race. But my money goes on him.'

'Take mine too, Uncle Pete,' said Victoria, handing over an orange note.

Uncle Pete raised an eyebrow at it, but then threw up his hands, saying, 'OK, it's your money if you want to waste it.'

Victoria only sent her thoughts flying towards the little dark horse and the dark man riding it, and said to herself softly, 'You just win, Shad.'

And that was what he did!

She felt boneless, her legs like unset jelly with the excitement of being involved in this sport which she had never participated in before—because she had been involved. She *had* wanted the Namangilla colours to come first. Victoria was glad when it was over. She told herself she wouldn't make a racegoer. But she laughed at Uncle Pete's face when he handed over her winnings.

She also decided she had had enough. A headache was the last thing she wanted before that Ball tonight, and what with the heat, the noise and the excited, jostling crowd all around her, she decided that could very well happen.

So, deciding to stroll leisurely back to the hotel, she turned away from a still-euphoric gathering waiting for the last race and was stuffing her winnings any which way into her handbag when a hand reached out to guide her behind an empty shed. She knew whose hand it was, of course she did! She found she couldn't speak as she stood there so close to him. However, Scott could.

'I've been intending to speak to you, Victoria, about that affair at the swamps. I simply haven't had time to spare for coming to the Leiths'. And I also had to have time to cool down. Because I had every right to be furious with you, but I needn't have——'

Interrupting, Victoria said quickly, 'It doesn't matter. I shouldn't have gone in there.' As it had done on the day which was the subject of their discussion, her hand went out entreatingly. This time it was taken.

She gazed down at it clasped in those hard brown fingers, and drew a deep breath before she continued, 'In a lifetime, one is allowed to make just one or two bad mistakes; so I'm counting that as one of them.'

Incredibly, Scott was laughing at her as she had come to know he did sometimes laugh, his body shaking with soft, silent mirth. Her own body relaxed as she felt the hand he was holding gripped more tightly.

'You shame me, Victoria! As if I hadn't made more than just one bad mistake in my life. However, I'm being selfish in bringing you my apology. Home isn't as it should be, with both Shad and Bobby looking at me sideways nowadays. . .' Scott's words trailed off, and for a moment they stood beside the empty shed, both silent.

There might have been silence between the two forms standing so close as they looked at one another, but from all round there was noise swelling. It seemed that the last race was in progress.

Then that wicked pirate's smile that her companion sometimes used surfaced, and a soft voice said, 'You'd better not be caught here with me.' A hand flew out in a casual gesture to the empty secretive space about them. 'You'd have no reputation left by nightfall, I promise you.'

Imagine him saying such a thing! she thought, puzzled.

But when she spoke it was with more than a little tartness. 'Don't be silly, Scott. No one—at least in the sense I expect you mean—could have a reputation ruined in today's world. Not with men and women sharing accommodation for all sorts of reasons—sex and sleeping together not being the only one.'

'Oh, and have you shared such accommodation?'

Unexpectedly, the atmosphere in the small cul-de-sac separating them from a people-crowded racecourse changed. Scott's voice had changed too, taking on that silken cadence she had already found denoted trouble. Unsure about this whole altered atmosphere which had come about, she gazed up at him, for that tone had sent a *frisson* of coldness through her nerve-ends.

'No, I haven't! But that was because I had other accommodation. As you told me once, I remember, there are always alternatives!'

'Yes, indeed there are, and we'll have to talk about them after the weekend. And,' here a low chuckle escaped him before he continued, 'you might be the only one talking to me by then! Shad and I probably cleaned up the whole district on the big race.'

'You didn't clean up as far as I'm concerned. Of course I'd bet on Shad,' said Victoria.

'Oh, would you? What if it had been me riding Dark Secret?'

'Oh, is that its name? And you know very well what I would have done, but. . .' It was Victoria's tone that had changed now as she asked, 'Was it what someone called a ring-in, Scott?'

Scott laughed, and the sound echoed carefree about them. 'Of course it wasn't,' he answered. 'Up here, you ride whatever horse you own—thoroughbreds, racing hacks, brumbies even. The animal Shad rode today was running wild, but by the way he *could* run he must have some sort of thoroughbred lines in his make-up. Didn't he go beautifully?'

'He certainly did!' replied Victoria, remembering.

'OK, then, I'll be off, my apologies given, and I'll see you tonight at the dance.' A hand was raised and he had moved out of their retreat with that silent predator's tread of his.

Absently standing where Scott had left her, Victoria became aware then that the last race must be over, the shouts dying away as people began to wend their way homewards to prepare for the second big highlight of the weekend.

She had better start doing that herself, she thought, and as she walked away from this shadowed place in which she had received an apology she had not dreamed of getting she decided she would look forward to the rest of this weekend. It could be regarded as a magic time that might bring other things so much wanted in its train.

So, catching up her shower gear, Victoria made her way through a hotel which was coming alive as the racegoers poured back into it. Because this was no luxury motel and the bathrooms were just an ablutions block; you took your bath when you found a shower empty.

Back in her room, she packed the pillows against the headboard and leant against them, dreaming. She stared at her dress hanging there beside Jennifer's on the outside of the wardrobe, and was glad that she had packed it— her graduation dress.

From a neckline slit low to a gathered-in waist, it fell free in swirling yards of chiffon, its colours changing from palest jade at the waist to a deep emerald-green at the mid-calf hemline. It was like, she had thought when buying it, the exquisite, unique shades that painted the ocean at Surfer's Paradise.

She was staring at it, smiling, still dreaming of a man who had spoken to her in that silken voice, when Jennifer entered in a tearing hurry. 'You'd better get showered, Victoria,' she exclaimed sharply, as she gathered up her own clothes.

'Oh.' Still smiling dreamily, Victoria answered, 'I've had my bath. Should I start getting dressed?'

'Not in that!' said the younger girl, indicating the shimmering dress swinging on a hanger. 'Not for dinner. The dining-room will be crowded and you could get a plate of soup, or more likely, seeing it's race-night, a jug of beer spilt over it.'

'But——'

'Victoria! You won't be eating in an expensive, exclusive restaurant tonight. You'll be among a euphoric crowd intent on enjoying itself. Put on anything, then come back for that.' A throwaway gesture indicated the lovely dress. 'You can do your make-up if you like. No one's going to spill soup over that.' Laughing, Jennifer departed.

So Victoria swung herself off the bed and picked up her brush. Sweeping up one side and the back of her hair, she fastened it in curls to the crown of her head. The other side she twisted into two long bangs, allowing some tendrils to escape and lie free.

Happy with that effect, she smoothed in a blue-green eye-shadow the exact shade of her dress. Then with a couple of swift strokes of a blusher highlighter, she was finished. Lipstick could be added after dinner. When Jennifer returned, Victoria followed her example and slipped into a strapless sun-frock and briefs. She decided that if it was going to be such a free-for-all, no one was going to notice how she was dressed—or undressed.

Arriving in the dining-room, they eased their way between closely packed diners to squeeze into chairs being saved for them at a long table. Victoria found herself between John Hamilton and a pretty dark girl who, she was thankful to see, was not Joanna.

She enjoyed her dinner among this youthful group at their end of the table. This was their big annual affair and they intended to make the most of it. There was laughter and jokes about other race days flying round; there was still a night's dancing in the offing. . .and they were young and careless and the world was theirs.

In the event, she didn't have a plate of soup or a jug of beer spilt over her. But someone else did, by the noise of a resounding crash which came from crowded tables at the other end of the room. It was followed by shouts of laughter, so it seemed that tonight everything did go.

Laughing themselves, they decided it was time to leave, so, squeezing among tables, among people and waitresses, they eased themselves out of a still overflowing and very noisy dining-room. Beside Jennifer and Peter, Victoria walked round the front veranda, then continued on by herself along the side one, when Peter pulled his companion over to the railings to speak to her.

Treading the hard wooden boards in her soft white slip-ons, Victoria smiled happily to herself—with euphoria of the day just ending, and the anticipation of a night yet to come.

She walked within a few yards of her room, and halted abruptly as if walking full tilt into a thick glass wall she hadn't known was there. Further along, away from the faint illumination of lighted rooms and dim overhead lights, stood two figures. Even as she looked, the man put both hands at the waist of the woman standing so close. He spoke, and Victoria couldn't discern the words which were almost inaudible, but the voice uttering them was familiar—so familiar.

And then, before she could make herself move, Joanna had stretched two arms up to clasp behind Scott's neck. The watching girl saw that beautiful face raised as it too offered all that her close-pressed body was presenting. Then the man, moving, looked across into her eyes, as she stood there, rooted. That glance broke the spell, freeing her. And in two jagged steps Victoria had gained the sanctuary of her room, closing the half of a french door which had stood open.

Blindly she made her way across the floor and sank down on her bed—against the still-banked-up pillows she had rested on before—dreaming.

Scott and Joanna! She might blame that deep conviction he had for not wanting to commit himself to a city girl. But he had said those special, haunting words about wanting her. . . And he had also told her once that he always only spoke the truth. So, remembering how he had consistently acted towards her, that meeting of just so short a time ago, she knew suddenly that he wouldn't be indulging in a casual affair out on the veranda. But. . .but Joanna was so exquisitely beautiful, and men often took what was freely offered—and it had been offered out there.

Victoria half raised herself. Almost silent footsteps were sending their vibrations along hard, weathered boards outside her room. However, before they could arrive, a cheerful voice called, 'Hi there, Scott. Looking for us?'

'No, mate, I was looking for Shad, but he's off

somewhere, so I expect I'd better get a move on to dress
for this shindig we all have to go to. So long.'

'I'll go along with you, Scott. Be back about eight-
thirty, honey,' replied the younger man, who sounded as
if he was sending a blissful smile across to Jennifer before
turning away. A pair of footsteps faded, one hardly
heard, the other echoing behind them until a corner was
turned. Jennifer came in and switched on the light.

'Oh!' she exclaimed, sounding surprised as she gazed
over at the supine figure. 'I thought as the light wasn't
on you weren't here.'

'I was just resting. I think I have a headache starting
from all that sun and noise today.' Victoria did think that
what she had just said was true too, and wondered if she
would use that as an excuse for not going to this dance
tonight. Suddenly she felt sick, and all she wanted was to
crawl away and hide. This diverse love-story of hers had
had too many ups and downs.

She could stay here and tell Jennifer so. That young
girl would most likely say, Oh, poor you, and be quite
indifferent about it. But she would tell her mother, and
Victoria didn't want Mrs Leith around here, fussing.

'You'd better get up and dress, Victoria,' Jennifer
interrupted these incoherent thoughts. 'I want to be there
when the music starts.'

So, sliding her feet off the bed, Victoria did get up and
begin to dress. The beautiful dress slipped over her
shoulders; she stood for a moment, then with a comb
carefully smoothed the back of her hair where she had
rested it against a pillow. Deciding that the rest of it
would do as it was, she stood back, murmuring. 'There,
that should do.'

Over her shoulder, reflected in the mirror, she saw

Jennifer's look and swung round. 'Don't you think it suits me?' she exclaimed.

'I can't get over it, Victoria,' replied her companion. 'You look a different person—a stranger almost, Like someone I'm just meeting; so different from the ordinary you I see around in jeans and T-shirt and casual cottons.'

'Well, thanks very much. I don't know whether to take that as a compliment or not. However, I'm pleased my hair's behaved as it should for once. It mostly likes to lie as I wear it, I've found out.' Victoria gave another glance into the mirror and satisfaction echoed in her next words. 'It *does* look sophisticated and other-worldly, doesn't it?'

'It sure does. But I'm pleased mine is nice and long, and with its natural wave doesn't need any fixing.' Satisfaction, as always with herself and her own plans, showed in Jennifer's words.

They were both ready when Peter's voice called through to them. He was outside, accompanied by Neil Paxton. Victoria smiled at this young next-door neighbour of theirs and then the four of them were walking towards whatever the night had in store.

CHAPTER TWELVE

VICTORIA saw that the hall was crowded as they passed through the cluster of masculine bodies congregated just inside the doorway. She grinned too, as did Peter, at the laughing comments he was receiving. Yes, she and Jennifer deserved them tonight. Settling down among their own party, Victoria only did what anyone else just arriving would do—glanced casually around the crowded hall. Yes, there was the shining gold head, among other fair heads. Scott was with the twins, lounging in his own indolent pose against a wall, speaking to the senior Mr Hamilton. Shad wasn't with him.

Then she saw him, sitting with people she had met from the mission, dressed as was Scott, and the majority of men, in the almost uniform of white long-sleeved shirt and tie. Coats and jackets might be around somewhere, but it was too hot to wear them. Her attention abruptly brought back to her own surroundings, she saw Neil standing before her and heard the music. The Race Ball had begun.

If she had thought Neil Paxton was a shy young man, she certainly didn't think that about his dancing. She found she needed all her concentration to keep up with him. He was good!

During one stop, before clapping restarted the music, she found herself beside Scott and his partner. He said, 'You haven't met Bronwyn Hamilton yet, have you, Victoria?'

Victoria smiled at the other girl, saying, 'Hi.' About

sixteen or seventeen, she decided, and fair like her
brothers, but without their looks and charisma. That
didn't seem to bother her, however. Contentedly, happily, she returned to the brotherly embrace into which
Scott drew her as the music restarted. But back beside
Mrs Leith, Victoria was interested in someone else who
was not being treated by Scott with only brotherly
attention.

'Oh, that's Laurel Seaton,' answered her employer.
'They have a station beyond the Hamiltons'. She's beautiful, isn't she? And spoilt. . .and likes Scott!'

'Don't we all?' muttered Victoria with acid softness,
remembering another scene on a veranda just minutes
ago. As that memory slid through her consciousness, she
saw Joanna enter the hall.

Like the last time she had seen her, this time too she
was linked closely to a man, her arm twined tightly
within his. The head above her didn't glint golden,
however. It was a nondescript brown, and if the air-
waves about him didn't exude charisma, they did hold
authority and assurance. Before Victoria could ask
another question, Jennifer exclaimed with dislike,

'Oh, there's no doubt about her. That's Dr Frank
Wilson, one of the Flying Doctors. I wonder what's
happened to Scott?'

'If she isn't with Scott, depend upon it, it's because he
doesn't want her to be,' replied her mother. 'And really,
Jennifer, I'm glad of that. Joanna wouldn't suit me at all
as my next-door neighbour—although. . .' Mrs Leith
laughed before continuing, 'I'm afraid that with whoever
Scott does marry, I'll have to learn to live with it. He's a
law unto himself.'

As she took all this in, Victoria's glance followed that

beautiful, eye-catching figure in its scarlet, floating crêpe-de-chine, with the shining ebony hair outlining the exquisite face. Any man would want her.

Then, alarmingly, Joanna and her beauty were wiped completely from her mind. Standing before her, a man was saying, 'My dance, I think, Victoria,' and like a sleepwalker she went into his arms. He danced as he rode—perfectly. He didn't speak, and she let herself follow effortlessly where he led. Once, inadvertently, she moved closer into the hard body guiding her. . .and found herself swung sharply away. 'Stop it, Victoria!' said that soft voice above her. 'Half the eyes in this room will be looking at us—a new girl in town, and dancing with me.'

She didn't care, and as she danced she wondered abruptly about this thing called attraction—love! Other arms around her were just that—arms to guide her about a dance floor. But that was not the case now. Nerve-ends sent out their message from every part of her that his arm was touching, and she thought that whatever was to come this night of enchantment, this dance in Scott's arms, would always be there to remember.

Startled, she glanced quickly up at him when he said, 'Well, thank heaven for that!' as the music stopped.

'What a dreadful thing to say!' answered Victoria, distress at his words showing.

'No, it's not,' Scott was walking her off the floor as he spoke, his demeanour casual, matter-of-fact for anyone watching, his fingertips barely touching her elbow. 'I've always been in command of any affairs I've been involved in, but I seem to have not one damned say where we're concerned. I'm giving in! I'll see you after this weekend and we'll sort things out one way or another.'

More than startled now, Victoria went to reply, but

found herself back in her seat. Scott said, 'Save the medley for me,' and was gone—as he so often damned well was, she thought angrily.

After that she danced with everyone who asked her. The swinging floor was the best she had ever danced on as they quickstepped and jived, and also waltzed in the old-fashioned way. After midnight, as time moved towards one o'clock when the Race Ball was scheduled to end, they polkaed up and down the slippery floor, breathless, laughing, to finish it all up with the hokey-cokey.

Waltzing with Shad in the dance he had come to ask her for, Victoria smiled up at him as he said, 'I've no need to ask if you're enjoying your first Race Ball in the never-never, Victoria?'

'No, you haven't! However, I could wish. . .'

'Didn't I say to take one day at a time,' was his answer. And then it was a few minutes to one o'clock and the medley. It was announced. As before, she went into Scott's arms when he held out his hand.

She was dancing as she had been all night, but even if the arm about her was loosely held it was Scott's arm. Then, as time had the habit of doing, it passed on its way. The music finished with the fanfare of a long-drawn-out goodnight and wouldn't resume despite the clapping, then once again she was being walked off the floor.

This time, however, towards a group of people already standing. Jamie Hamilton, an arm round the beautiful Laurel, greeted them. 'Dad's laid on champagne and eats in the small lounge at the hotel. . .and I want to talk with you, Scott. I haven't been able to get hold of you since that damned race, and I want to know all about this ring-in. It's no good asking Shad—he just smiles with all his

teeth showing and doesn't answer. If John and I didn't
know differently, we'd think he was dumb. But he could
certainly talk when he wanted things done on that
outback station of ours.'

'A ring-in? Surely not,' interrupted a deceptively soft
voice. 'He belongs to Shad, and is duly registered.'

Mr Hamilton laughed, saying, 'Well, come along.
We'll have a drink to toast him—always hoping he
doesn't win next time.'

They trooped out of the hall, and, walking between
Uncle Pete and Scott, Victoria saw that their numbers
were growing. Joanna and her doctor were among them.

Outside, she thought that although there might be a
vast empty land around them, there was not silence.
Voices called, laughter and talk echoed still from groups
reluctant to finish this night, and Victoria, walking
between her two escorts, glanced up. The stars were
brilliant, scintillating diamonds, and yes, lower down,
there was the Southern Cross, familiar, and a part of
home. While it shone above she was in home country.

She walked up the shallow steps with no helping hand
to guide her. Around in the small lounge, champagne
had been laid on. It was being opened and passed around
by the twins. Victoria stood back, nursing the glass John
had brought to her, content to just be there listening to
the flow of laughing abuse which practically everyone
was indulging in.

Scott, not Shad, was bearing the brunt of most of it,
but Victoria grinned, uncaring. He could more than hold
his own.

Then unexpectedly he held up a hand, palm outwards,
demanding quiet. He glanced across at the hotel owner
and raised half a dozen fingers. Receiving a nod, he
swung back to face the room. Victoria wondered what

was coming—something outrageous, she decided, noticing even across the space between them the way those sapphire eyes were gleaming, that pirate's smile widening.

'I'm tired of being blamed for Shad's wrongdoings——' Perforce Scott stopped against the shouts of derision coming from all sides. Shad of course only stood there, saying nothing.

'I'm tired,' Scott was repeating, 'of all this unfruitful talk about our little Dark Secret—so I'll give you something else to discuss.' His glance swung round the room and abruptly the noise died down, all eyes on him, wondering what was coming.

Champagne bottles were being opened again, this time by the hotel owner, and as glasses were refilled Scott said, 'I hope you'll be happy to drink to my engagement.'

No one answered, his words not really penetrating. Then Scott reached out a hand and said, 'Victoria.'

She couldn't move. . .but she could have killed him. Then he was walking across to her and, taking her hand, turned to face them all. It was the senior Mr Hamilton who broke the astounded hush.

'Congratulations to you both.' He raised his tall glass and drank before adding, 'May you have long life and happiness.'

The room was suddenly in turmoil, but through it all Victoria heard her name said loudly twice, in a tone of incredulity by Mrs Leith, and in a far louder scandalised tone from Jennifer.

Congratulations were pouring in from all sides; Scott's shoulders were being punched, but more than a few puzzled looks were being sent Victoria's way. She didn't care. They could think what they wanted! Then a streak of coldness did penetrate the excited, laughing voices about her. Frank Wilson stood before Scott, hand out-stretched. His companion's murmuring words Victoria didn't catch as she stood with her arm again twined tightly with that of her escort. Joanna was certainly playing the beautiful, adoring woman, desired and wanted by an attractive, attentive man.

Someone else was murmuring quietly as the crowd around them dispersed a little. It was Mr Hamilton. Again, Victoria didn't catch what he said, but whatever it was Scott showed pleasure by his answer. 'Thank you, sir. Yes, if that could be managed, I'd like it very much.'

It seemed only minutes after—but must have been more—when Scott said to her, 'Would you like to go and change out of that finery, Victoria? We're going for a drive, and I wouldn't dare have that spoilt.'

'Would it get spoilt, Scott?' she asked, not caring.

'It damned well might. Where we're going, I'd feel more comfortable with you out of it.'

She stood staring, and then his words must have registered. Laughing naturally, he told her, 'I didn't mean it to sound like that! However, as far as I'm concerned those words could be only too true. Go and change!'

So she went away, moving thankfully into an older group who were departing. It seemed, though, that that was not going to be the case with the younger generation. It looked as though they intended to make a night of it.

Safely in her own room, with the designer creation smoothed on a hanger and the previously discarded sun-frock slipped on in its place, with high-heeled sandals changed for casual slip-ons, Victoria decided to transform the elegantly attired woman dressed for a special evening completely. So, reaching up, she slid out her hairpins and, shaking her head, sent her hair tumbling down in a cascade of shining disorder. She combed it straight. There, she decided; that's me!

Dressed, she stood for a moment, wondering where she should go. Not back to that room in which Joanna had stayed. But she found she didn't have to wonder. Scott was lounging against the railing opposite her door. Across the few yards separating them, she looked at him. . .and felt her bones melt, her body's metabolism shatter into immovable fragments.

Was this because Scott had now declared himself? she wondered incoherently as that gaze still remained locked with hers. Then he moved and the spell was broken.

He guided her, not towards the front of the hotel from where the sound of merriment was sounding out in full swing, but out through the back where there were vehicles and tents scattered about, some silent and dark, some with occupants still intent on enjoying what was such a special day up here.

Victoria walked through the warm night—no, the early morning, hand in hand with him. It was so unreal! Walking hand in hand with Scott had never, ever entered her thoughts. He just wasn't the kind of man one would imagine behaving like that.

She noticed that the stars seemed to have lost some of their brilliance, and without thinking asked, 'What's the time, Scott?'

He didn't glance down at a watch he didn't wear. He squinted up at the sky and then towards the horizon. 'About three-thirty or so, I should imagine. A little over an hour to daybreak. Here, up you get.' His fingers were withdrawn, but his hand was held out to help her up the high steps.

Victoria settled into what was becoming a familiar corner, and watched as he slid behind the wheel with that easy fluid twist with which she was also becoming familiar.

They seemed to be driving for a long time, and the flying night outside, the close confines of the little cabin, began to take on the atmosphere of a dream. Would tiredness from the crowded day just past account for that? she wondered hazily. She put out a tentative hand to touch the dark-clad leg stretched out beside her, then as carefully withdrew it. Scott wasn't looking at her because of what she had done. He had pulled the Land Rover to a stop, saying, 'We're at journey's end, light of my life!'

The dreamlike quality vanished completely, and she answered more than a little acidly, 'Yes, I can just imagine being the light of your life.'

Amusement and the careless echo of laughter showed in his voice when he answered, 'Come along out and we'll sit in the back and watch the dawn come up.' He pulled the large rear door open and, with his hands under her arms, swung her up to sit on the floor. He jumped up to settle beside her, saying, 'Now, Miss Victoria Steene, about this engagement. . .this marriage of ours. You do want to marry me, don't you?'

'You know I do—of course you do. But to do what you did! It would have served you right if I'd said, "Whatever do you mean?"'

'Why didn't you? I'd have deserved it. But it had to come out some time, and unexpectedly I decided that then was the time. There were so many other things to distract their attention.' Scott had picked up her hand and was rubbing a thumb up and down it absently. She tried to pull it away, but only found it clasped more firmly.

Suddenly she laughed, thinking of either the stunned silence, or the resounding uproar among all those friends of Scott's if that had happened. She replied, 'You knew I wouldn't, of course. But when you did make that outrageous announcement, even standing across the room from me, you looked so different that I thought you might have been drinking—and good heavens, that wouldn't have been so different. Every man and his dog were drinking tonight.'

'I don't drink—it's not one of my failings. But I have more than enough of others. A violent temper being among them—but then I have Shad to keep me in order. Now—we have to talk seriously. I know. . . I realise. . .women should have the say about the time and place of their wedding. However——' that voice, normally so assured—or silken-soft in some situations—showed uncertain hesitation now '—do you think you could marry me today fortnight?'

She thought she hadn't heard aright at first, then she exclaimed, 'You must be mad! In two weeks? What about my parents. . .? What about. . .oh, a million things?' Then enlightenment came. 'You don't want to go south. You want to get married up here, but I can't, Scott. . .'

He didn't answer, and that absently stroking thumb was working its own magic. Victoria thought of all that going home for a wedding would entail; she thought of herself showing Scott off to all her friends, and knew it all didn't matter. Only one thing did matter!

So, taking a deep breath, she said instead, 'As long as I marry you, Scott, I don't care where I'm married. My mother won't be happy about it—and I *would* like to show you off, saying, "Look what I found up in the never-never!" Oh, Lord, we'd have the gold-rush days all over again.'

'Flattery will get you nowhere at the present time, although I take leave to inform you that I will be open to it later on. Do you truly not mind being married up here?'

'I've told you. However, my parents would want to be at my wedding, and as you've so acrimoniously told me more times than I care to remember how isolated this far north is, just imagine my father on that slow train to Chillagoe. Oh, heavens!' uttered Victoria, aghast at the very thought.

'Oh, that!' Scott waved away such a trivial subject. 'There are planes galore up here. Any or all of them will be laid on. Now—to more important things.'

His arm around her, that thumb apparently absently moving up and down taking more than half her concentration, he said what he had once before, and in that soft, silken voice it took on the cadence of a promise. 'More than anything I want to make love to you. . . More than anything I want to have you completely in my arms. However. . .' With a finger under her chin he turned her face to his, and when his lips came down on her own they were not demanding, not bringing them both to that plateau of want, need, that his lightest caress could evoke; they were gentle, feather-light.

Because this was Scott, she went to meet that caress with her body arching into his, moulding herself into the curves and hollows that made of them one entity.

He drew away, saying, 'Look, Victoria, I know what making love to you does to my control. Tonight, allow me to inform you, control and tiredness are a bad combination. It wouldn't take much for me to throw everything to the wind. Only,' the breathless, hurrying voice was continuing, 'when I do make love to you completely, after all these on-again, off-again scenes of passion and desire we've been through, I want the leisure of time on my hands. So, as we're to be married in two weeks. . .'

Victoria remained still, immobile. She had only to reach out a hand and touch him—she knew that! She moved carefully and sat up straighter. She said, 'OK, let's go home,' and edging towards the open door she jumped down by herself—and stood transfixed. 'Look, Scott!' she breathed.

Straight out opposite, across the greyness of vast distance, was a crimson line. Not the mass of ordinary vivid colours that a sunrise splashed across a horizon; this was as if a pen had been dipped in scarlet ink and with a ruler had drawn, incredibly straight, a line of deep crimson.

Scott had also dropped down and was placing a loosely held arm about her. 'Yes,' he answered, and the word was softly spoken, 'I have seen it before. It's one of the reasons for this drive up here after the long day and night just past. I needed to get into familiar territory. Too many things have been piling up on me, and this,' he threw out an arm in a throwaway gesture, 'brings it back into perspective for me. So. . .' He turned her to face him in the dim light of a false dawn that was slowly turning into violent daybreak, and continued, 'Let's go and face that mob back there, and in a fortnight, I promise you. . .'

'Promises, promises!' Victoria laughed up at him, and for the first time she stood on tiptoe and kissed him of her own accord. 'Did you mention something about tiredness? With only two weeks to manage all we will have to do, tiredness might become the operative word!'

It was Scott who laughed this time, out loud, sending the sound echoing into the empty bushland about them. 'That's my girl!' he said. 'But didn't I just give you a promise? I won't be tired then—believe me!'

CHAPTER THIRTEEN

IT WAS irritating her, and Victoria turned away from the touch. But her shoulder was shaken again, and a voice said, 'Victoria, Victoria. . .'

She knew she had tried to push her eyelids open, but she could see nothing. She wanted to burrow again into the pillows, but the voice said more loudly, penetrating the haziness, 'Victoria, wake up!'

Startled by the curt words, she jerked herself upright. Bright sunshine was outlining the open door, and across from her Jennifer was also sitting up in bed. It was Mrs Leith standing looking down at her that drew her attention.

'What. . .what time is it? Is something the matter?' she was beginning, when abruptly last night and its happenings flooded back into her memory.

'Sorry, I've slept in,' she was still continuing, but the older woman was waving her words aside, saying,

'Is it really true, Victoria?'

Before she could reply, an exclamation from the other bed carried across to her. 'How can it be?' queried Jennifer. 'Victoria's hardly been in his company except for that one trip to Chillagoe.' Suddenly her eyes flew wide as she looked Victoria over. There was no prize for guessing what she was thinking.

Drawing the deep breath that she needed to answer that knowing gaze, Victoria found that she was being pre-empted as her employer said, 'Scott wouldn't do what he did unless it was true. Is everything all right,

Victoria? Is it what you want?' Mrs Leith paused for a moment, then said hesitantly, 'I do feel some responsibility for you, you know. Your mother entrusted you to me when you came up here!'

'Yes, Mrs Leith, it is truly what I want, and it's certainly not what Jennifer seems to think. To set your mind at rest I'll tell you that I fell in love with Scott practically the night I arrived, when he walked into your kitchen.'

'You couldn't have, Victoria!' Scorn showed in Jennifer's voice. 'Good heavens, you didn't speak to him, and he didn't even look at *you*. I remember, because I'm always careful of Scott when he's around.'

'You're right on both counts, Jen. But there was an attraction between us right from the start.' Victoria wasn't going to mention that first meeting on a far distant railway siding. It would only complicate matters and call for further explanations.

Happily, an exclamation from Jennifer interrupted her. 'How on earth can you consider marrying Scott, Victoria? It would be absolutely the last thing I'd do. Sometimes that look he gets. . .' Jennifer shivered.

Yes, Victoria knew she was right. Scott did sometimes have a look that made one walk warily. Living with him wouldn't be all a bed of roses—but living without him and the love and desire he could evoke wasn't a thing to be thought of.

She was smiling at the memory of some of those times and turning towards the older woman, when her glance was drawn to the open door. A man standing there had just raised his hand to knock.

Victoria pulled herself further up in the bed, pushing her tousled hair from her face, hearing Mrs Leith speaking to Scott, 'I couldn't like it, coming out of the blue last night. I didn't know what to say or think. . . But this morning. . .'

Their visitor gazed at this woman he had always known, and smiled carefully. Before he could answer, however, Mrs Leith had walked the few steps separating them and reached up to kiss his cheek. She said, 'I do wish you happiness, Scott.'

A tinge of red came to colour his smooth, tanned cheeks and, delighted at this phenomenon which she had never dreamed of ever seeing, Victoria grinned. He said only, 'Thank you, Mrs Leith,' and that lop-sided smile with which he had received her congratulations returned to the normal unrevealing nature of his everyday one, before he added, 'Do you think I might have a word with Victoria? I'm going to be up to my eyes in phone calls soon and I need to do some checking first.'

'Of course.' Mrs Leith moved away.

Jennifer said, 'If you think I'm going to get out of bed with you standing there, Scott Courtney, you have another think coming!'

'And if you think, Jennifer Leith, that I haven't seen women with much less on than you'll be showing, *you* have another think coming!'

Victoria's hand flew to her mouth. Heavens!

But Scott was only gazing at the younger girl, and suddenly Victoria could understand what Jennifer had said a moment ago about that look he could get. It wasn't the laughing pirate's gaze she had seen him sometimes wear when he was sparring with her. It held cold, chill ruthlessness. Abruptly, in the warm sunshine, Victoria shivered. Then she thought, This is Scott, don't be silly!

Unexpectedly, Jennifer threw back the bedcovers and stalked out to join her mother, short nightdress and all. Scott came across and sat on the side of her bed. Gravely she returned the look he was directing at her. She said, 'It isn't fair,' as she attempted to push some sort of order into her dishevelled hair.

His hair, citrine-yellow, showed slicked back, still damp from the shower, and his skin showed no glint of unshaved gold this morning—only smooth bronzed symmetry. But his eyes held a tiredness lurking in their cornflower-blue depths. 'What isn't fair, light of my life?' he asked. 'You have no need to worry about lying there on your pillows looking as you do. I hereby inform you that I'll be very happy to have you in my bed every morning, looking exactly like that.'

It was her turn to have that tinge of red flooding her cheeks, but there was astringency coupled with acid in her reply. 'I don't understand you, Scott. In all the months we've known one another, you've never used an endearment—except once, and that could have been called a special time—but now, and in these circumstances. . .' Her thrown-out hand indicated the rumpled bed, the small unlovely room.

'But, light of my life,' he answered, and it wasn't a careful smile he was wearing now. She recognised that wicked, piratical one which came into his eyes when he was thinking, or preparing to say, something outrageous. 'You weren't my affianced bride then. Society allows so much more leeway when that's the case. Are you happy to be my affianced bride, Victoria?'

'I was.' She paused, thinking she would have to learn to hold her own with him, then went on, 'But after that suggestive remark to Jennifer just now, I'm beginning to have second thoughts.' She added, without being aware of having remembered them and in the same tone, the two words Scott had used to her while laughing at one of her tirades, only transposing his name for hers. 'Really, Scott!'

'Jennifer's spoilt rotten; she needs her little bottom smacked, hard! Now, about these phone calls. . .and arrangements. Lord, aren't there always arrangements? I'd like to just pick you up, get away to Townsville and get married on our own, but I know I can't.' He gave her a lop-sided smile. 'No?' he asked.

'No. With most things I'd say yes to you, Scott, and if it was necessary I'd agree. But one has to go on living afterwards, and that would hurt my family.'

'Yes, of course. . .' A low chuckle erupted from him. 'But you really can't blame a bloke for trying, now can you? You don't know what it's going to be like. Arrangements are being put in train already.'

'I expect I can't, Scott,' she was replying to the first part of his sentence, when the second part hit at her. 'What arrangements are being put in train?' Her voice was almost a squeak.

'You'll find out. Everyone seems to be getting into the act—the Hamiltons first. That's where we're getting married——'

'Did Mrs Hamilton suggest it?' interrupted Victoria, remembering the distant, haughty woman who hadn't had a great deal to say to her.

'They both did. She might look, and act, a trifle forbidding at times, but I owe her as well as Mr Hamilton a great deal. You'll find,' here that smooth, tanned face opposite her broke into a sardonic smile, and an eyebrow went up, 'that they'll put on a fairy-tale wedding for us.'

'A fairy-tale wedding will be a bonus, Scott. As far as I'm concerned, as long as one particular groom is there, I'll be satisfied!'

Scott threw up both hands and said forcefully, 'Oh,

I've had enough of women this morning and the things they say to me, but the time will come when I'll be able to reply in kind. In fact it's coming along quite swiftly. . .so watch yourself!

'For now, however, to business. It's damned strange how things work out. I knew I'd have to go south fairly soon on some legal affairs. So if I can hurry up the work on Namangilla, I'll meet you in Brisbane for the weekend you're there.'

'Just a weekend?' Her voice rose in dismay.

'Victoria, we're patching things together as we go along. Understand me—I want this marriage in a fortnight. It would be senseless to put it off to allow time for this to be done, or that to be accomplished. . .'

The soft, low voice paused for a moment, then resumed. 'First things first, which is to phone your parents. The police station is the only phone connected to Chillagoe, and it's only used by outsiders in an emergency. We're treating this as an emergency—for favours given—so meet me there at eleven.

'Oh, and we have to go to that barbecue afterwards, don't forget. Even if I haven't got time I'll have to make it; I couldn't allow you to go like a Christian to the lions by yourself, because this afternoon you must realise that everyone, but everyone, will be coming along to congratulate us.

'I'll also have you know that it's my turn to say it isn't fair,' he added. 'Until you came up here to disorganise my life, I planned it out and it did as it was told! I can just imagine that barbecue this afternoon. . . Still, we'll face it when we come to it.

'Eleven o'clock,' he repeated, and rose to go.

'That's fine,' said Victoria. 'They'll be home from church by then. Oh.'

'Now what's the matter?' On his way to the door, his attention plainly on other things, Scott sounded irritated.

Tentatively, a little slowly, she asked, 'How are we getting married, Scott? I mean, by whom?'

He shook his head. 'Good heavens, Victoria, I don't ask a woman to marry me without knowing something about her! Father Robert from the Bush Brothers. OK. . .?'

'Yes, OK,' was all she answered, but she thought, I love you, Scott Courtney, but sometimes, so help me. . .!

'I'll see you at eleven, then.' He flipped his hand, then he had turned and was gone. Once again she was gazing at his disappearing back; a situation, it seemed, that she would have to get used to, if she was to live with him.

She swung her feet out of bed and went to meet Jennifer and her mother. 'I have to shower and get round to the police station,' she told them. 'Scott has arranged for me to ring home,' she explained. 'Is that all right with you, Mrs Leith?'

Receiving a nod, she swung away, knowing she was late. Then, showered and dressed, she went out into the bright morning. Scott was waiting with the sergeant. Nobody else was there, she saw thankfully, knowing that everything she said would probably be overheard.

'Give me your mother's number, Victoria. We'll get it now.' In only seconds, it seemed, Scott was handing the receiver over to her. But in even that brief touch of his fingers, even in these circumstances, she felt the electricity that always held them together catch and hold. Then her mother's voice was saying hello.

'It's me, Mum,' answered Victoria, and cut through the delighted torrent of words. 'Look, I'm on an official phone, so I can't talk for long. I just rang to tell you I'm engaged! Yes,' she interrupted the reply, 'to be married.'

She turned her back on those satirical blue eyes watching and said, 'Yes, I am. Yes. . .he is.' She was trying to keep her replies as short as she could, very aware of the two men waiting—and listening.

'Yes, look, I'll go into all that later. I'm coming down to Brisbane on Monday or Tuesday. I'll ring you from Townsville, and Scott's coming down for the weekend, so you'll meet him then.'

'Promises, promises!' Victoria heard the words she had said to him not long ago quoted *sotto voce* behind her. But the phone was quacking again into her ear.

'Look, Mum,' she answered hurriedly, 'we'll talk when I get down there. But I was wondering if in the meantime you'd look around for a wedding dress for me. You know what would suit me.'

She listened again, then replied, 'No, not a long dress and veil. Mid-calf length, I think,' and added, after taking a deep breath, 'We're being married on Saturday week.'

This time the line wasn't quacking, there was a dead silence for several seconds. Then Victoria was replying, 'No, the only reason is that Scott asked me to. And yes, I accepted. Yes again, he does have a job.' It wasn't Scott she heard this time; it was the police sergeant's snort of disbelief, but she carried on regardless. 'He owns a station next to the Leiths'. Look,' she found herself saying for the tenth time, 'I'll see you soon and you'll meet Scott then. OK?'

As the next question echoed across those thousands of miles of telephone wires, she gazed helplessly at both men, then said flatly, 'Yes, I am in love with him!' She put the receiver down on the still-talking voice.

'You'll come and meet them, and you'll be on your best behaviour,' muttered Victoria through clenched teeth to the fair-haired man smiling ironically at her, both eyebrows raised this time. I have to do things I don't want to do, for you,' she told him wrathfully.

Both his hands went up, palms outward in the universal gesture of peace. 'OK, OK,' he replied. He said thank you to the sergeant, and added, 'I have things to do, Victoria, but I'll be there to take you to the barbecue in half an hour or so.'

Victoria didn't go looking for Mrs Leith at once. She went back to her room, packed her case, and knowing what she was going to be in for later looked herself over in the mirror. Thank goodness she had chosen to wear this sundress. It was almost as lovely as her ballgown—if in a different way. From a white band just above her bustline, it followed the curves of her figure to flare out below in tangerine silk. It also showed off the apricot tan that living up here had given to her skin. Then she went to find Mrs Leith.

It didn't turn out to be such an ordeal after all. Scott took the brunt of all the comments and ironical remarks being sent their way. And *he* could look after himself. Oh, couldn't he? thought Victoria, listening.

It was Shad, however, who came to her, holding out a packed-up plate as he said, 'Come over into the shade with us, Victoria. You didn't have any breakfast, and you must be starving.'

Unexpectedly, amazed, she found that she was. It hadn't been only breakfast she had missed. Last night at dinner, she had been thinking too much of what the night might bring to eat much.

So now she sat under the welcome shade of a gum tree and ate all her lunch. She gazed about her at the young people as they sat indolently in canvas chairs, lounged on rugs outspread on the grass, knowing the whole world was theirs. She listened absently to their talk and laughter. . .and felt herself becoming a part of this community; this sunburnt country.

Far back in her mind, dredged up from a forgotten reading in her university days, part of an Arabic quotation surfaced. 'It is here! It is here! It is here!' Yes, it *was* here where her happiness lay.

Then Scott's presence was at her back. He smiled at her as she turned to look up at him. It was his fingers moving smoothly back and forth across the nape of her neck which had told her he was there. She felt the shiver that passed through her whole body.

Then they were gone, and he had found a place to fling himself down on the grass at her feet. He was talking to Jamie Hamilton, waving a greeting to someone coming across from the group surrounding Joanna, who was holding court there. She *was* holding court too. Another doctor from the Royal Flying Doctor service had arrived to add his presence to the group around her. John Hamilton was there also with a short, cheerful dark man with whom Victoria had danced last night, and who was trying to make time with the blonde, beautiful Laurel. Now there were two women who complemented each other. Both would cause men's heads to turn for another look.

Thinking that, Victoria turned her glance away, and gazed carefully at another fair head which almost rested against her knee. She wondered why Scott hadn't. . . Then told herself not to be stupid. He had always known both lovely women, and if he had picked herself, being Scott, she was what he wanted.

Unexpectedly, his glance swung upwards and she was looking fully into his eyes. She felt her cheeks burn. Her thoughts, those secret thoughts, must have been exposed naked for him to read.

Below her own quickly swung-away head, she heard his voice speaking casually, normally, aware that she would not be able to take command of her senses so swiftly. Abruptly she hated him. She wasn't that important to him, she decided angrily. Or he wouldn't be able to act as if that look between them had not occurred.

Then her glance caught sight of his hand down on the grass beside him. Those long fingers were closed into a fist, showing white beneath deeply bronzed skin from the force of a tension within.

Suddenly, shatteringly, the scene around her was outlined in brilliance. She *was* what Scott wanted, and she would go forward to meet whatever came, knowing also that with him everything wouldn't always be a bed of roses.

Then he was rising, and laughing across at the twins said, 'I've got to go and get my little Dark Secret home. Look after my girl for me, but keep your cotton-picking hands to yourselves, you understand?'

'Would we dare do anything else, Scott?' The words came from both youths simultaneously. Then Jamie added, 'Of course we will, and I won't tell you to enjoy yourself down in the big city when you get there. I'm afraid that for you, my friend, those days are gone forever.'

Scott only laughed, then, raising a hand to them all, he touched Victoria lightly on the shoulder and walked away.

What a leavetaking! But that was for public display. In private, it was an entirely different matter.

CHAPTER FOURTEEN

'COME on, Victoria, wake up!'

She heard the familiar words, felt the shake on her shoulders, and she was back in Einasleigh the morning after Scott had taken her on that drive and had talked marriage plans with her.

She flew up in bed, and saw then that it was still dark and that her fluorescent dressing-table light was switched on.

'It's going on four o'clock, Victoria. Tea will be ready in five minutes. Hurry now,' Mrs Leith was saying.

'Yes, OK, Mrs Leith.' Victoria swung out of bed, and felt the butterflies that tumbled and fluttered beneath her ribcage. She knew why they were there. Today was Tuesday and she was going home to face her parents, and she would be married to Scott in ten days.

Showering and dressing, she tried to keep only practical matters occupying her mind. Certainly not to remember last night! Scott had arrived to fix new arrangements. Because the Hamilton plane had been full on Monday, she was going with Mrs Leith today. Scott was travelling tomorrow with Mrs Hamilton, who was going to shop for the wedding, she had declared forcefully.

After finalising arrangements about accommodation for her parents with Mrs Leith, he had said, 'Come and see me off, Victoria.' So she had walked outside and stood by the gate at which his horse was tethered. He had drawn her away from it into the dark shade of a big gum, and with an arm about her shoulders had said quietly,

'The underpinning of the house is finished, and we start on the roof tomorrow. Practically all the outside will be completed before the wedding, but you're going to take forever refurbishing the inside.'

'Am I really?' replied Victoria, but she said it absently. She could hardly see his face in the darkness of the tree shadow with just starshine to bring it illumination, but she had thought he looked tired back there in the brightly lit kitchen. 'There's really no need to rush the work on Namangilla,' she told him. 'How many hours a day are you putting in?'

This time a low laugh echoed before he said, 'Dare I say twenty-four? But I'll have those three or four days in Brisbane to loaf.'

'That's what you think,' answered Victoria tartly. 'I can just imagine what will be lined up for us there, but still, we'll be going away after the wedding, so you can loaf then.'

No reply was forthcoming for a long moment, then Scott said, 'Oh, yes, the wedding,' and suddenly, out of the blue, she was in his arms, held tightly in a prisoner's grip.

He was bending her backwards, her hair cascading in a fall across his arm. Then, slowly, sensuously, he was pacing his way down the exposed column of her throat until those passion-laden caresses were halted by the soft lawn of her blouse.

For a long heartbeat they remained there, then his lips had moved to search their way across bare silken skin before coming to rest on her own. Pulling a hand free, Victoria slid both arms up to lock behind his neck, and so they stood, bodies fused into one, while burning, devastating kisses showed her the need of a desire too long kept in check.

Then that fair head above her lifted, and he pulled her to lie against his chest. She remained there, immobile, while the rapid, thundering heartbeats beneath her cheek slowed. Scott's voice when he spoke showed none of the nuances with which she was familiar. 'That's what I wanted to do up on the ridge the other night,' he said, 'but I knew that if I started there'd be no turning back. However, here,' a low, shaking laugh sounded, 'I knew I'd be safe. If we stay out here too long we'll have Mrs Leith calling out for us to come back and have a cup of tea.

'But, Victoria, until Saturday week I'm keeping away from you, and from empty spaces under dark, concealing trees. For now, I'm off. I'll see you in Brisbane.' He was gone, stepping from stirrup to saddle in one easy fluid movement. Then all that had come back to her was the swiftly moving clip-clop of hoofs as they went from a trot to a fast canter.

So now she drank her tea, ate the hot buttered toast, and as an impatient honk came from outside for the second time went to collect her case and then on out to where the big Jaguar was waiting.

It was dark, the sky shining with stars, and she thought she would have to get used to these early starts. They seemed to be a fact of life up here.

'How long does it take to get there, Uncle Pete?' she asked their driver when they were on their way to the Hamilton station where its owner was to fly them to Townsville, then listened only absently to his answer as she remembered that the next time she would be at the Downs she would be going there to be married to Scott.

She had wondered about Scott's reaction to all these plans being made without his say-so. He was not the kind of man one took liberties with. However, Mr Hamilton had waved her worries aside, saying, 'We owe Scott on Jamie's account. We look on him as one of the family, and it will be our pleasure to have the ceremony at our place.'

So Victoria could only reply, 'Of course, Mr Hamilton,' but somewhere in the back of her mind she was wondering what her parents were going to say about the wedding being held, not at Scott's station, which they would have accepted, but at the Downs, given by people they didn't even know. Oh, well, it was all out of her hands, so now, with the hundred-odd miles the wheels of the big Jaguar would have to slide behind them, she settled back to try to remember also the hundred or so things she had to do.

The sun came up and she watched it rise until it was no longer a big red disc but a golden ball of fire. Then cattle grids were rattling beneath them, and fences making their appearance.

They drove past the house when they arrived—a big place, Victoria noticed, but not a beautiful old colonial homestead like Namangilla. They came to a stop beside an airstrip where a plane was already warming up.

'Hi,' said its owner. 'You're five minutes late, Pete.' They smiled at one another, these two elderly men who had probably always known one another.

Victoria sat behind the pilot and watched the land below slip away incredibly fast, thinking how vast this country beneath them really was. It was still, however, with incredulity that she glanced at her watch when Mr Hamilton turned round and said to the two women, 'Townsville coming up, tighten your seatbelts.' It was just eight o'clock. Planes *did* make a difference.

Beneath, the city was rushing to meet them, but Victoria didn't even feel the bump as they landed. Out of the plane, walking across the tarmac and into the airport building itself, Victoria found her ticket waiting. She also found that all she had to do was wave to Mrs Leith and the tall austere man beside her, then they had both turned to go about their own business.

She took a deep, steadying breath, thinking that she was on her own now, with the arrival at her own home to be treated as a matter of course and put behind her. In the rest-room before her boarding call was announced, she made up her face carefully, knowing she would need some assurance. She thought she looked older.

She picked up her big shoulder-bag and returned just in time to hear her flight being called. She slept all the way to Brisbane.

'Darling!'

'Hello Mum.' Victoria looked at her mother and smiled, all her tension draining away. This was the loving woman she had always known. What had she been worrying about?

However, the older woman was saying, glancing at the jeans and T-shirt Victoria was wearing, 'You don't look dressed to go shopping—at least, not where we're going shopping. But time being of the essence, as you told me in your hurried phone call, we'll go and see how your wedding dress is coming along.'

'OK, wait until I get my bag. There it is!' Victoria grabbed at her case as it materialised on the carousel, then followed her mother.

Car key in hand, Mrs Steene paused for a moment, then swung round to face her. 'Victoria,' she said, 'this wedding is very sudden, and being married up there instead of at home. . . Are you sure—happy about it? Because we're here, you know, if you need us, your father and I.'

Victoria almost found herself using Scott's 'Really, Mother!' then pulled herself up. What should she answer? She found herself saying, 'I am in love with Scott, and——'

'Never mind, then. We'll meet him soon and see for ourselves—he's coming to dinner tomorrow night. Now come along and shop, because for what we have to do I'd like time to stand still for a couple of days. It won't, of course.'

So they went shopping. Victoria tried on her half-finished wedding dress, shaking her head at her mother as she stood while it was being pinned. It wasn't a clear white, but the faintest of ivory, and not fitted at all. Falling from a yoke tight across her bust in a frothing swirl of chiffon, it could have been copied from a Regency print. Even its tiny puffed sleeves, edged with the narrowest of intricate guipure lace, brought to mind the same era, and it was exquisite.

She told her mother so, once it had been slid back over her head and carried away. 'You have the most fantastic dress sense, Mum. I'd never have found anything I could love more.'

'No, I don't think you could,' came the complacent reply, which went on to say, 'Irene's is in the palest lemon.'

'Is it upsetting her schedule being my bridesmaid at such short notice?' Victoria asked. 'I realise everything just can't be put down at a moment's notice——'

'It *is* a short time,' came the interruption almost tartly from her mother, who seldom spoke like that. 'I simply can't see any reason for it.'

'Yes, I know, Mum,' Victoria was suddenly grave, and when she was dressed again she added, 'Scott didn't want to wait. . .there was simply no reason to.'

'You'll have to tell me—and your father—why he thinks that. You said he had a station, but not what kind of one. If it will support you. If. . . Well, never mind for now, we have shoes to buy, and another outfit!'

There was more than one outfit, Victoria found. However, finally they were on their way home.

There, among the rushing, nerve-racking, peak-hour traffic, Victoria found that while her mother's attention was on her driving she could tell the story of her on-again, off-again love-affair with Scott. It was almost finished when her mother swung the car into the garage.

'Look, Victoria,' she was informed firmly, 'all that's as it may be. But this young man is after all only a young man, personable and attractive as you claim he is. Still, you've been living in a land where there are probably not a great many attractive men. Perhaps down here, among company you've known and mixed with, things will fall into a different perspective. *Now* what's the matter?' Her mother's words had come sharply.

Victoria had begun to laugh while thinking of Peter, kind attractive Peter, and the Hamilton twins, outstanding in any company, and Scott. . . Heavens!

She said, 'Maybe you're right, Mother. Look, we'll just wait until you meet him, then you can see for yourself.'

So the next evening—after another frantic day of co-ordinating every little jigsaw piece to meet and tighten together into one united whole—while she waited at a window overlooking the drive, her mother's words caused her to swing round and gaze at herself in the mirror above the mantelpiece. She *was* in a different environment; she *did* look different.

Would Scott think her so? She smiled back at her reflection. It didn't matter what he looked like, what he would be wearing. She would have to take only one glance. . . Her breath caught. She swung away from the mirror, from the strangeness now of a pleated silk skirt, a white lawn blouse with sleeves full and puffed into the wrist. Beautiful, tailored. . .they *were* different. They were not jeans and T-shirts or casual cottons, which was the attire of the far north, except for special occasions.

She heard a car, and now saw it, big and dark, as it swung into the driveway and came to a stop. Then with the smooth, fluid movement that she remembered, the driver stepped out. He bent to extract two long boxes, then walked towards the open door.

Victoria didn't notice what he was wearing. She knew she had held out both her hands in greeting, but that only one was taken. She looked into those familiar eyes and abruptly their two figures stood locked together. Her own lids fell, and without meaning to, without thinking at all, she swayed towards him.

'Really, Victoria!' said that easy, pleasant voice, and her eyes flew open. She gazed down at the hand he was holding, then up at him. She saw then that, like herself, he was dressed differently.

Gabardine trousers fitted his lean hips as if they had been tailored for him—as they probably had been—with a jacket of the same material, unfastened over a cream silk shirt. 'You'd better come inside.' Reaching out to them, her mother's voice broke the spell, and, obeying it, Victoria used her free hand to shut the door.

Then suddenly the space about them came alive, movement and talk echoing as her father and sister entered and were introduced; red roses handed to her mother, golden yellow daffodils to her, accompanied by a *sotto voce* murmur as they were passed over, 'Roses are not your flowers, light of my life.'

Knowing she would be unable to answer with any degree of composure, Victoria went away to find a cream vase. Filling it with the daffodils, she took it along to her bedroom, feeling Scott's glance following her until she was out of sight.

She sat at a crystal- and silver-laden table and ate the tempting food her mother had prepared—and listened while her father asked questions about the far north. She also heard the polite, careful answers he received.

Then at last her mother said, 'Why don't you take Scott for a drive, Victoria, or go for a walk in the garden? You'll probably have quite a few plans to discuss.'

Glancing across at him, Victoria felt her relief at this suggestion suddenly evaporate. Damn him, she thought, he shouldn't do this! Because for the first time tonight, Scott was looking at her with an expression of not merely polite interest, but with a pirate's gaze colouring his sapphire eyes. Then abruptly her tension eased and she smiled over at him, saying easily as she would have done up at the Leiths',

'Yes, we certainly have,' and, rising, she led the way outside. 'Do you want to go driving?' she asked.

'No, I do not. I don't know my way around this madhouse—and, although you might, I'd prefer a walk in the garden.'

She was being drawn close to him, and on tiptoe, arms clasped tightly about his neck, she knew this was where she belonged; where her heart and home resided.

Remaining there, she said huskily after a minute, an hour, an aeon of time, 'If I feel like this after only a few days away from you, how am I going to feel when you and Shad go touring around your far northern boundaries. . .to the big musters?'

The familiar ripple surged through the body what was

part of her body, and, still laughing, he told her, 'We might have to take you with us. How about that? However, before we return to this real world we happen to be in, and plans that have to be made, I've a private plan of my own to put into action.'

So, amid the wafting fragrance of a garden awash with summer flowers, his arms came to claim her, and as she had in the Leiths' garden, in a different country two nights ago, Victoria collapsed into him, allowing his kisses, his caresses to roam where they would.

At last, when there was no garden around them, when only fires of desire and passion coloured the world, that bright citrine head lifted. With lips lifted from the ones he had just plundered, he said, that silken, easy voice of his sounding strangely breathless and shaken,

'Come over here and we'll sit down properly and make those plans.' He indicated a wooden garden seat just yards away. Even through the clamour of her passion-hazed senses Victoria thought, as she did so often about this man, that he would see it there, darkness notwithstanding.

He took off his jacket, placing it around her shoulders, and the soft murmur of the two voices echoed quietly through the sleeping garden.

CHAPTER FIFTEEN

THE slender figure in the large bed came slowly awake, and as on another occasion so long ago, bright sunlight outlined an aperture. Although it was a long window, not an outside doorway, it brought back memories of a man standing in the bright opening with a hand upraised to knock.

No one was standing there this morning, but there was a man sleeping on the pillows beside her. Sideways, Victoria glanced at the exposed face resting there. She made no movement; she didn't want to disturb the sleeper. She knew from past experience that he invariably caught any emotional air-waves emanating from her—some of which she would rather keep to herself.

She closed her eyes quickly, cautioning her body to stillness. Opening them again, she noticed that the tanned face was almost as dark as Shad's now after two weeks away with other station owners sorting out a big cattle-duffing operation. The whole affair had erupted the day they arrived home, and of course Scott had had to go. A lot of the stock had been recovered, the rest shrugged off. Cattle-duffing was a fact of life up here; you won one, you lost one.

The molten rays, however, of six weeks of sun, four of them on the beach and in the ocean as well as the two just past, might have darkened his skin, but they had lightened the citrine hair, shading it from its normal hue of gold-yellow to the even fairer colour of silver-gilt.

Involuntarily, Victoria reached out a hand to smooth

away a fallen lock of glittering brightness, but caught it back swiftly. She didn't want him awake—not yet. She had things to think about, and words to get into order.

It had been a crowded two weeks before the wedding— every day of every one of them. She had not seen Scott after their dinner at her home. She had shopped. . .and shopped! She had flown back up here on the Saturday laden with cases of linen, with new clothes for a trousseau, with her wedding dress.

She had found Namangilla homestead still not ready to move into, although the outside was nearly finished, and had surveyed, impressed, the vividly painted paving tiles of the newly created back entertaining area.

Then her family had arrived—to find Scott away. Driving them over to Namangilla, she and Mrs Leith had shown them around, and leaving her mother and sister with her erstwhile employer talking curtains and paint colours, Victoria had gone outside to stand beside her father.

She asked as she watched him look the lovely place over, 'Do you like it, Dad?'

He smiled his cool smile at her. 'Who wouldn't? You know, we were worried about your coming way up here to live, but now. . .' He shrugged, then continued frankly, 'It's not only this, is it, my girl? It's the man to whom it belongs?'

In her turn, Victoria glanced all about her, then replied, 'I expect, Dad, that this is a plus; but yes, as far as Scott is concerned, he could have nothing and I'd be like Ruth in the Bible, go anywhere as long as I could be with him——*Oh!* How long have you been there?'

Anger and a furious indignation showed in her last sharp sentence. Her father swung round. Scott was standing a few yards away. He must have left his horse

in the stockyards, because he was dressed for riding—
and he was filthy.

Beneath the layers of dust, he smiled at her, at them
both. She wondered if he had heard what she had just
said. . .then smiled too, sardonically, at herself. Of
course! Being Scott, he would have. He had the habit of
knowing everything about everything—at least where it
concerned him.

'Hi there, Mr Steene. I'm sorry I wasn't here to
welcome you, but needs must when work calls, as in your
profession you probably know,' he greeted her father.
Then, turning to her, he said, 'I expect it's just as well,
Victoria, for you to see now what you're getting into.
Dirt, mud sometimes. . .and. . .' He flicked a hand at
his unclean person.

'I've seen you dirty before, Scott, when we were
mustering. I know what goes on up here. Also, I might
have been wrong, but I thought I saw a washing-machine
out there, and the power to work it.'

Victoria knew she was babbling, wondering what her
father would think of those words of hers which had been
so unexpectedly interrupted; wondering what Scott
would think. Suddenly she didn't care. He had no right
to be there behind her when she had spoken as she had
of him. A girl needed to have some secrets. How many
times had she used that word 'unfair' as applied to him?

Indignantly she turned and walked quickly away,
leaving the owner of all this, dirty and caked with dust as
he was, to look after her father, while she went inside to
make herself talk curtains and paint with the three other
women.

It was Shad, who apparently had made time to shower
and change, who came looking for them. Tea was ready,
he told them, and with his slow smile guided them out to

a big gum shading one part of the new barbecue area. A table was placed beneath it, and Old Bill and Bobby were already present.

Victoria had been worried about how her parents would get on with this family of Scott's. She found she need not have been. There came laughter and questions; there was dark fruit cake and delicious scones with home-made jam.

Scott, showered now as well, golden-yellow hair, sapphire-blue eyes drawing all their glances, had arrived and was putting himself out to be charming—and when he wanted to be charming, just couldn't he be! thought his bride-to-be acidly. She also thought that *she* had never been on the receiving end of that charm now being distributed around so freely.

Of course, everybody liked Shad, and her father's questions kept him busy. She noticed her mother gazing thoughtfully at the exquisite china they were eating and drinking from, at the silver tea service, and shrugged. From what she had seen when Bobby had been hurt, and she had been so unexpectedly and drastically drawn into this household, this sort of paraphernalia was always used—whether in the house, or under a tree in the open air. She had more important things to worry about.

One of those important things was suddenly in evidence. Bobby had come to lean against her as he had done at other times. She smiled down at him, saying, 'Hi there.'

However, his little face remained grave. 'Will you mind teaching me, Victoria?' he asked worriedly. 'Scott said the other night that it was a good thing you were coming and thank goodness for you and your teaching ability! Shad laughed so funnily at him, he laughed and laughed!'

Victoria bet she knew why Shad had laughed. Her teaching ability would have been a non-event in Scott's scheme of things, and Shad would have known it.

Still, that was one thing she could take off his shoulders, allowing him that extra time for the outside. So she smiled down at the little boy as she told him, 'Of course I won't mind, love. We'll manage very well, because Geoffrey will have gone away to college by then. However, one day it might be better if you go away to school like all the other boys from up here. Would you like that?'

'Yes, I expect so, because I know you have to go when you're bigger.' His gravity and worry gone, he smiled up at her happily, and she brushed the hair away from his eyes while returning his smile. Abruptly, as she had on a far-off picnic day, when doing the same thing, she knew she was being watched.

She met Scott's expressionless blue gaze, and with haughty upraised brows turned away. She had got over being flustered by him and the way he could look, she told herself tartly.

The sun was on its way to the horizon by the time her family was ready to leave. As she saw them off, Scott's hand held her back, guiding her behind a screen of rioting purple bougainvillaea. He pulled her to him, his body pressed hard against hers, and his mouth came down, scorching, unexpected.

Then as his lips lifted and his head came up, she heard him say, 'I've been thinking of doing that for a whole week. Have I ever told you I love you, Victoria? And—oh, lord, that I want you!'

She could only hear her heart thumping. She knew she had to go out and face those watching eyes in a few seconds' time. She was aware of what her face would show.

Then Scott was laughing down at her, eyes contracted into gleaming diamond pinpoints. He said, 'What does it matter, Victoria? Come along, let them guess what I've just done.' He took hold of her hand and, swinging it, walked her over to where the cars were waiting, speaking as they went.

'I'm dining with you tonight at the Leiths', did you know? Jamie's flying over tomorrow to take me back to the Downs for what they say is going to be a bucks' party to end all bucks' parties. Peter's going too, and Shad, of course.

'However, I think the twins have some idea of getting me roaring drunk. They have Buckley's chance and their own! I don't even like beer, which is almost an impiety up here in the far north. Still, I have a lot to thank Mr Hamilton for, and with Mrs Hamilton really laying it on for the wedding. . .' He hesitated as if going to say more, but remained quiet as they drew near the waiting group beside the big Jaguar.

Victoria replied, trying to speak just as casually, 'I know about the dinner, and your party, because the twins should be thinking of going back to university. They wouldn't, of course, miss your wedding for the world.'

It seemed no one was going to miss the wedding. It seemed everyone in the entire north was going to be there. However, later that night, sitting across from Scott at the crowded dinner table, Victoria saw that unlike this afternoon behind the bougainvillaea screen, he was going out of his way to keep himself, and his glances, from her vicinity. She didn't wonder why! Although it was uncalled-for, and definitely unwanted among all these people, she still felt stretched between them that invisible line of a tense emotional strain.

Then, of course, amid frantic last-minute preparations, cases packed, dresses donned, came the actual morning when she was being married to Scott. She had been told, and she knew, that she looked lovely; that her dress was beautiful as it floated around her in shimmering, swirling folds. She gazed down at it as it spread about her on the seat and smiled at her sister, 'You look lovely, too,' she told her, and received smugly back,

'Yes, don't we both?'

The plane was touching down, close to the waiting cars. Her mother was straightening the half-wreath of cream frangipani, seeing that it was securely fastened to the back of her hair. Mrs Leith was doing the same for her sister with frangipanis in her hair too, the golden centres matching the colour of her dress.

The taped wedding march was swelling out, and Victoria was walking on her father's arm through what seemed crowds of people to where two men were waiting. They were also looking unlike their usual selves in formal grey. Then she was standing beside one of them, who turned and looked down at her—and smiled! Unexpectedly, the haziness, the dreamlike quality of the whole frenetic morning had fallen away, and the minister was saying, 'Dearly beloved. . .'

They had been married for six weeks now, with a honeymoon on the Gold Coast for four of them. Victoria remembered once on one of their tours glancing up from sipping champagne to see Scott's eyes fastened upon her. He had turned quickly away, but not before she had seen a strange expression in his look. She had moved away from the group she had been speaking with, and walked towards him.

'Isn't this a fabulous trip, Scott?' she asked.

They were travelling the waterways among beautiful houses and twisting canals, and today was the last of their tourist outings. It was a fantastic trip, and Scott had been laughing and happy. So what had suddenly brought that queer expression to those dense blue eyes?

He answered her, still with that expression showing, 'I've been watching you and thinking how much at home you are in all this.' His hand went out in a throwaway gesture to the scene around them, to the lovely buildings and gardens lining the glittering waterways through which they were passing.

Victoria shook her head. She told him tartly, 'Yes, I am at home here, and yes, I do come from the city, but oh, heavens, wasn't I lucky. . .so lucky that I went to a job in a place called the never-never? Scott, you are my life!' She turned quickly away and upended her wine glass, swallowing the lot in one gesture.

A hand had reached out and long, tanned fingers were suddenly entwined with hers. She swiftly blinked back tears and said with a laugh, 'And aren't I lucky as well that I'm getting a home called Namangilla that puts all these in the shade?'

This time it was Scott who was laughing, that strange expression wiped away. He said in that silken tone he only used sometimes, 'I don't know if I'd say that—some of these houses are out of this world. However, to change the subject, did I ever tell you that I love you?'

She didn't need to answer; she sat there on a seat running the length of the boat, their clasped fingers hidden between their two bodies, and thought back on the last four wonderful weeks. Tomorrow they were on their way home. . .

Now, this morning, her thoughts about the wedding, and her honeymoon, were abruptly gone with the wind. She went rigid. The immobile form beside her had moved, and an arm snaked out to pull her to him.

'What,' asked a soft voice, 'has my secretive wife been thinking of for the past hour?'

'It hasn't been an hour, and you were asleep.'

Again she felt that familiar silent ripple of laughter contract the hard form so close beside her. One lazy blue eye went towards the long opening which led on to their own private veranda. It took in the turquoise arch which showed a sun that had already climbed well above the horizon.

'And what would I be doing asleep at this hour? I realise it's Sunday, and that I don't work on that day if I can help it, but lying in bed with the sun where it is. Really, Victoria. . .! Still, leaving work aside, I expect there are other things to do.'

His lips came down and rested on the corner of her mouth, then began to travel downwards as they always did, with a hand coming to rest where it always did in the hollow of her hip. Unable to resist those lips, that hand, her body obeyed their message—then halted its flow into the completeness of his as she remembered. She pulled away and said breathlessly,

'I was only thinking about our wedding. Mrs Hamilton outdid herself, didn't she?'

'She did at that! We'll have to think of something spectacular to do when one of the twins or Bronwyn gets married. But for now, Victoria, what is it?' In a different timbre, Scott's voice asked the last question quietly.

'What do you mean by asking what is it? I was only thinking.'

'Oh, come on! Don't you realise by now that I know every nuance of your voice, every response that your entire metabolism makes to me?' Scott finished speaking and his hand moved, the fingers trailing from the hollow below, over the midriff, across suddenly aroused breasts, to come to rest against her throat.

Up on an elbow, gazing down at her, he asked again, 'What is it?'

Swinging away from the subject she really wanted to discuss, but was finding it difficult to do, Victoria said, 'Isn't it marvellous that Peter and Jennifer are getting married and that they'll be coming to live even closer to us than Mrs Leith does?'

'Victoria! I know about Peter and Jen, and the house, because Peter consulted me first. I also know, although you might think it's a secret between you three women, that there's a plot afoot to have a large saucer installed that will enable television to be beamed down to us from that Assat satellite. Now, what is it that's worrying you?'

The last sentence came flatly, and suddenly there was a new tone in her husband's voice, and she didn't like it. She said hurriedly, 'All right. Do you remember that night in Brisbane when you had dinner at home, and we sat out in the garden afterwards and talked?'

'If you must know,' came the soft, uncompromising reply, 'I remember *every* scene and encounter with you. What's so special about that one?'

'Well, you began to discuss marriage and how it would affect us——'

'I did!' She was interrupted, and Scott was continuing on forcefully, 'Because it should have been discussed long before that. You must admit, however, that ours has been no ordinary courtship. Also, I thought that coming from a houseful of doctors you'd be aware of all you'd need to know——'

'No, it hasn't been an ordinary courtship, has it?' In her turn, Victoria interrupted, then paused. Waiting only so long, her companion spoke,

'Keep to the point, Victoria. We still haven't got to what seems to be worrying you. As you do sound so apprehensive, however, I'll tell you there's only one thing you could have done that needed all this roundabout rigmarole you've been going through, and I don't expect it's that, so. . .'

Victoria cast a glance at the man now lying flat beside her, one arm flung above a tousled gilded head, blue eyes hooded to cover any feeling they might have held.

'Well, you said to me once,' her words tumbled out more than a little breathlessly now, 'that you supposed a girl should have some say when her wedding day should be. So I expect,' the words were coming even more swiftly as if she wanted to finish them. 'So I expect,' she repeated, 'that a man should also have some say about when he wants to become a father!'

Abruptly, there was a different dimension emanating from that immobile figure lying so close. No words answered for a moment, then she saw the smooth, tanned chest rise once sharply, as if a breath had been taken.

'Yes, I expect that could be said to be the case,' was all he answered.

'Well, the occasion didn't seem to arise. You've been out chasing stolen stock since we arrived home. . .'

Again an arm was reached out and she was pulled into the shelter of a warm, hard body. 'Do you really mean to tell me,' said a voice with a quite strange inflection, 'that in all this time I could have been indulging myself more than I have been doing?'

Victoria's eyes flew wide, and she found she was gazing into a gaze of glinting sapphire. She asked carefully, 'You don't mind, then?'

'Good lord, Victoria, of course I don't mind, but you. . .'

'Oh, me?' She was laughing up at him, but found she wasn't going to be allowed to finish. Scott was kissing her with all the expertise he was capable of. She did hear him speak, but it didn't register. She moved her body even more closely into the hard, demanding one completely enfolding her own, flying to meet the desire and passion beating about their two entwined forms.

She gave herself up to those known hands, those caressing lips which were sending the sunlit room, the very space around her into a far world as they went, bodies and minds soaring together, to the very centre of the universe.

Later, but how much later it was she had no idea, she heard Scott saying in a tone sounding unlike any one of the several she had at times heard him use, 'Did I say to you—oh, an aeon or so ago—something about indulging myself? Do I owe you an apology for that wild exhibition just now, Victoria? For not being aware of what I was doing or where I was going? Or do I say once again that more than anything I love you; more than anything I want and need you?'

Answering, the still lingering haze of blind, blazing passion making her own voice strange too, she said, 'Do you really, Scott? You can always be my guest, you know.'

Then, into the stillness and silence enclosing the space about them, knowing that she should, Victoria moved and spoke, 'Is it very late? Because I suppose that even on Sunday, although we don't work, we have to eat. . .or you men do.'

'OK.' Scott slid out of bed, and she heard the shower running in the adjoining bathroom. Back, standing by the bed, looking down at her, he said, 'Stay there, I'll bring you some breakfast.'

Only a glance of amazement answered him while she replied with her tone carrying more than a little tartness, 'Really, Scott!' then added, 'Yes, I did come from a house of doctors and I know what my brother who *is* in this line of medicine would say of such behaviour. I'll be out in a few minutes.'

She went to swing out of bed, then hesitated as Scott remained gazing down at her. Unconscious of the automatic gesture, she pulled the sheet up. Scott grinned, a raised eyebrow going sky-high. Then, his glance roving the tumbled, disordered bed, he said in his turn, 'Really, Victoria!' He shook his head and departed.

Once again, as she was becoming used to, she found herself gazing after that disappearing back. Then, showered and dressed in a pair of skimpy yellow shorts with top to match, she grinned back at herself in the mirror, at the slim silhouette, the apricot-tanned long legs. She had better wear these outfits while she could, she told that reflection, and laughing, she swung round to leave their bedroom.

Her husband of six weeks was finishing his breakfast when she entered the glassed-in veranda where they ate now, except for formal occasions. He rose and seated her, pushed close the glass of freshly squeezed orange juice and poured her tea. 'You look beautiful, light of my life,' he told her.

Victoria glanced suspiciously over at him.

'Truly,' he said, mimicking the word she so often used, then added, 'I'd better get out there before they cut down all my orchard. Shad says that tending the food we eat isn't working, so I'd best go and do my share.'

He came round, and, bending, dropped a kiss on the nape of her neck under the tied-back brown hair. And even now, even yet, she felt that shiver Jennifer had once mentioned pass down her spine.

Finishing her breakfast, she still sat on, chin in hand, dreaming. Her head came up as a shout of laughter came echoing from outside. Rising, she glanced down at the disordered table—and left it with a grin.

If Scott could indulge himself—well, so could she. So, walking from the homestead of Namangilla, she went out to join the working party among the fruit trees.

She raised her glance from the busy scene before her to gaze at the deep azure arch above, then dropped it to look further into the distance, where even at this early hour it was hazing with the heat. Yes, this was where she belonged.

Then, as a voice called, she looked over at them, all three of Scott Courtney's possessions, and went happily forward to add herself to their number.

Next Month's Romances

Each month you can choose from a wide variety of romance with Mills & Boon. Below are the new titles to look out for next month, why not ask either Mills & Boon Reader Service or your Newsagent to reserve you a copy of the titles you want to buy – just tick the titles you would like and either post to Reader Service or take it to any Newsagent and ask them to order your books.

Please save me the following titles:		Please tick √
THE WEDDING	Emma Darcy	
LOVE WITHOUT REASON	Alison Fraser	
FIRE IN THE BLOOD	Charlotte Lamb	
GIVE A MAN A BAD NAME	Roberta Leigh	
TRAVELLING LIGHT	Sandra Field	
A HEALING FIRE	Patricia Wilson	
AN OLD ENCHANTMENT	Amanda Browning	
STRANGERS BY DAY	Vanessa Grant	
CONSPIRACY OF LOVE	Stephanie Howard	
FIERY ATTRACTION	Emma Richmond	
RESCUED	Rachel Elliot	
DEFIANT LOVE	Jessica Hart	
BOGUS BRIDE	Elizabeth Duke	
ONE SHINING SUMMER	Quinn Wilder	
TRUST TOO MUCH	Jayne Bauling	
A TRUE MARRIAGE	Lucy Gordon	

If you would like to order these books in addition to your regular subscription from Mills & Boon Reader Service please send £1.80 per title to: Mills & Boon Reader Service, Freepost, P.O. Box 236, Croydon, Surrey, CR9 9EL, quote your Subscriber No:.................................... (If applicable) and complete the name and address details below. Alternatively, these books are available from many local Newsagents including W.H.Smith, J.Menzies, Martins and other paperback stockists from 10 September 1993.

Name:...

Address:...

....Post Code:...........................

To Retailer: If you would like to stock M&B books please contact your regular book/magazine wholesaler for details.

You may be mailed with offers from other reputable companies as a result of this application. If you would rather not take advantage of these opportunities please tick box ☐